.40

the secret of the mountain

ESTHER LINFIELD

THE SECRET OF THE MOUNTAIN

Greenwillow Books New York

Library of Congress Cataloging-in-Publication Data
Linfield, Esther.
The secret of the mountain.
Summary: Follows the adventures of a fifteen-year-old Xhosa boy living in the cattle lands of south-eastern Africa as he undergoes the rituals to attain manhood and takes his place as a responsible member of his community.
1. Xhosa (African people)—Social life and customs—Juvenile fiction. [1. Xhosa (African people)—Social life and customs—Fiction. 2. Africa, Southern—Fiction] I. Title.
PZ7.L6623Se 1986 [Fic] 85-9912
ISBN 0-688-05992-9

Among those who so kindly gave guidance and suggestions, I am particularly indebted to the late Dr. J. Jolobe, Mr. L. Mbuli, Mr. P. Ntloko, and Mr. W. K. Tamsanqa of Umtata; the Rev. M. Maqashalala of Mt. Frere; and Mr. R. Matshongo of Matatiele.

I should like also to mention Eugène N. Marais' *The Lions of Magoeba*, which inspired an incident in this book.

foreword

In the midlands of south-eastern Africa, between the mountain highlands and the coastal plains, lies a well-watered country of deep valleys and hills. From a time far back in the past, this has been the home of the Xhosa people. Here, season after season, day after day, they have grown crops and tended cattle.

Long ago, land was plentiful, and the pastures were sweet for their herds. Cattle was their life. Cattle was wealth. To have as many as possible was their desire. A man could dream of herds so vast that the dust they raised would cover the sun.

Now the herds are small. The life of the people is changing. But some still follow the old ways, and tell of how it was before, when the fathers of their grandfathers were boys.

E. L.

the secret of the mountain

chapter 1

In the high, rolling country where his people lived with their herds, great hill after great hill was turning green, and the fields were fresh with the start of new grass. That day Anta and a few of the other boys had taken the cows to a small sheltered valley behind Nkomkobé Hill. The slopes stood in shadow over them, and across the valley the ridges of rough sandstone rose steep and dark against the sky.

All morning long they played games in the cool grass, keeping an eye on the cattle. "Where are you going?" they cried shrilly when any of the animals strayed too far away. At midday, when the sun was overhead, and the herd began to move to the shade of the thorn trees, the boys decided to go to the fields and gather sticky berries for their bird snares. They drew lots, the eldest holding a clump of grass in his hand, as many blades of grass as there were boys, and in drawing the blade with the knot on the end, it fell to Anta to stay with the cattle.

He was sitting and watching some cows as they grazed closely together near the stream when, from behind the dense plumbago bushes on the opposite bank, two strangers appeared, driving before them three gray cows. The men approached slowly and carried their sticks head down, almost touching the ground. When they reached the stream, Anta saw them drive their cows across, allowing them to mingle with his father's cows. The men remained at the side of the stream while their animals grazed among the other cattle. Suddenly one of them whistled sharply. Their three cows stampeded across the stream, bringing with them the rest of the cattle. By the time Anta realized what had happened, the men and the cattle had vanished behind the plumbagos. He ran out to the fields, shouting to the other boys to come back. Then he ran home. He could still hear the lowing of the cattle as they protested being taken away. How was he going to tell his father that six of his cows were gone?

He went directly to the hedge of the cattle fold, where he found his father, Khwane, sitting with his men, sharing a pipeful of tobacco. No sooner had he blurted out his tale than his father rushed into the great hut and grabbed a stick and a spear. Fighting sticks held high, the men rushed after him down the hillside.

Anta waited all day in the great hut. His father had said nothing to him, and he was afraid. It was not until nightfall that the men returned. He could hear them outside, talking to the women. They had followed the tracks to the edge of the forest, where they had discovered the cattle herded together in a small clearing. They had waited for darkness and then whistled their cows home.

"What boldness to take the cattle of a chief," said one.

"Those were Oba's men, the dogs!" Anta heard his father exclaim. He knew what this would mean. There would be a raid of reprisal, and raid would follow raid; so it had been for as far back as he could remember. Men raided for cattle and fought for cattle. Hardly a year of his childhood had passed without the sound of the war cry.

Anta and the other boys were up at sunrise to take the herds to the grazing grounds. Amid a commotion of shouting and whistling, a trampling of hooves and a lowing of cattle, they opened the gate of the fold and let the animals out. In long, leisurely files the cattle began to move down the familiar trail.

Near the foot of the neighboring hill Maboni joined them, driving his father's stock alongside theirs. Maboni—Anta did nothing without him. From the age of six, when boys first go off by themselves, he and Maboni had been inseparable. Together they had herded goats, hunted field mice, and trapped birds. Once Maboni happened to catch in his snare a little wagtail, a bird of good omen. They had buried it, placing two white pebbles in the grave for the ancestors, because to kill a wagtail was

3

a bad thing. No harm came of it, but the anxiety they shared for days, not daring to tell anyone, sealed their friendship. At fifteen years they were as close as brothers. Anta could not think of a moment in his life when he had not known Maboni.

At sundown that day Khwane was waiting for the return of the herds. Anta knew his father was never so happy as when he watched his cattle come home in the evening. From the cattle fold he could see them cross over the ridge and amble down in a slow, steady stream. Patriarch of his people, he stood by the hedge, resting his long stick across the back of his shoulders, his red ochered blanket a mantle around him. Hearing his long-drawn whistles, the cows parted from the herd and came forward to be milked by the young men. The herd went on through the open gate, and his father followed. He seemed content just to walk among them, to touch a warm horn and smell their sweet grassy breath. Then, abruptly, he left them and went to the cooking hut.

When his father hurried off after the evening meal, Anta knew that there was to be a meeting to discuss the matter of the stolen cows. He intended to find out what was going on. Many a time, after shutting up the cattle at night, he and his half brothers, Diko and Sidalo, had hidden themselves and listened to the men talk of the wars. But it was never an easy thing to escape Old Mother's sharp eyes. He would wait until the children began to crowd around her for stories.

His own favorite tales were those which she told about his father, Khwane, her son. A commoner by birth, he had first come to Oba, his Great Chief, to render services, as young men do, in return for food and a few head of cattle. He had stayed on, distinguishing himself by his bravery and his powers of oratory, for which Oba had made him a counselor and later a chief. Anta still liked to hear these stories. But now, as soon as the old one started talking, he slipped away and ran behind the men's hut, where he knew he would find Diko and Sidalo. Peering through a mud crack, he saw his father and his counselors sitting in a circle around the fire. As he strained to catch their words, he watched their faces.

He knew his father was gentle as well as brave and knew that he had no thirst for war. He sent tribute to Oba, attended feasts and ceremonials, and was often called to his Great Place. Anta knew, too, that his father had grown rich in cattle. "The size of your sleek herds do not please the Great Chief," a counselor was saying. Another suggested that the theft of the cows was pretext enough to break with him. But his father replied that the time was not right. Some of the counselors looked surprised, but Khwane stood up, and the meeting was ended.

In the sleeping hut Anta listened while Diko

spoke impatiently of the delay. Anta had a great regard for his oldest half brothers, Diko, aged nineteen, and Sidalo, eighteen. He had always wanted to be like them. How envious he was; how they astonished him by the number of things they knew. Not only did they know the color and markings of each one of their father's animals, but they knew their neighbors' cattle as well. They knew all the cattle paths and where they would lead, and they could tell at a glance what had passed that way before them. Of all his father's children, Diko and Sidalo were the ones he admired most.

However, his deepest affection was for his sister Nomaliso. She was twelve. When she was a little girl she used to cling to him, and she still tried to be with him as much as she could. Secretly he did not mind, but it brought him a good deal of ridicule from the boys. There was another bond between them: They were cattle-linked, paired by their father, so that one day the marriage cattle received for Nomaliso would be used to provide a wife for him.

Among the wives at home Anta liked the youngest, Tandeka, the best. She was cheerful and kind, and all the children liked to go to her hut for food. Sidalo's mother was kind, too. He was less fond of Thubisi, mother of Diko. She was the right-hand wife, next in rank to his own mother.

His father had taken his first wives while still a

young man, but when he became a chief, his counselors had chosen for him a wife who would be suit-
able as a chief's great wife. The wealthy men had
given liberally, and a dowry of two hundred head of
cattle had been raised for his marriage to Balakazi.
She was the daughter of a chief, thus of royal blood,
and as great wife she was the most important
woman in the land. Balakazi was called the mother
of her people. It was he, Anta, her first son, born
after three daughters, who was the main heir and
successor. Although his father was not noble by
birth, he had been ennobled by the medicines and
rites of chieftainship, and surely no one could look
more chiefly. He was tall, upright, lean as a spear,
and bore himself with dignity. His voice was strong,
and his step firm.

For days after the theft of the cows, the boys kept
the herds close to home. Then Oba summoned
Khwane to a meeting of counselors. Once more
Khwane obeyed his Great Chief, but when he found
that while he was away another cattle fold had been
raided, his resentment turned to open defiance.

On the day of the antelope hunt it happened that
Khwane killed a bluebuck. He immediately said that
he would not send the breast portion to Oba, who
demanded it of all chiefs tributary to him. Indeed,
everyone knew that Oba preferred the breast of a
tiny bluebuck to the choicest part of any of the larger
animals. When the news reached him, he sent word

to find out if Khwane would change his mind. Khwane refused.

Four days later Anta saw a messenger arrive at his father's Great Place, carrying a lion tail in his hand as token of office. Oba and Khwane were at war. Messengers came and went as arrangements were made for the time and place of battle. Diko was excited. Now he, too, would be among the warriors.

Khwane informed his headmen, and within a very short while the people had been told. From the hilltop the women of the Great Place gave the warning. Their piercing, ululating cry was taken up by the women of the neighboring places and carried from ridge to ridge.

As the call went out, men cleaned and sharpened their spears and the women prepared food for the journey. Anta saw the men as they began to arrive. They sat down in front of his father's hut, singing while they waited.

Then Khwane came out of his hut and stood before them. "The cattle have left us!" he cried. "Again, Oba and his cowardly dogs! Now it is war. The ancestors are with us. They will be fighting above our heads." Filled with pride, Anta listened to his father's voice ringing across the courtyard, as Khwane roused his men, praised them, and called them by the names of their ancestors.

They killed an ox for the ancestors because victory depended on them. The war doctor arrived. From the doorway of the hut Anta and Maboni saw him burn roots and herbs and pound them into powder, crush the leaves of plants and add their juice to the water in the pot. The warriors formed a half circle and stood in silence while he walked around swiftly, using a wisp of dry grass to sprinkle each man. The drops ran off their spears and the backs of their hands. The war doctor stirred another pot, taking omens. Anta waited anxiously until he saw that it had foamed up over the rim and the war doctor was satisfied that the time was right for battle.

The two boys went into the courtyard to watch Diko. He and the other new warriors were given their weapons. After this Khwane gave out the crane feathers that were to be worn by those who had been many times to war.

Throughout the day the ceremonies continued. Tens of cattle were killed so that the eating of meat would make the warriors strong and fit for battle. Long lines of women climbed the steep footpaths leading to the Great Place, carrying on their heads earthen pots full of a frothing brew. For days the army drank, danced, and feasted. Each morning Anta had to see to the cattle as usual, but at night he sat up late by the great fires that burned till dawn.

At last Khwane gave the order for the army to march, and wearing his headdress of blue crane feathers, he led his men down Nkomkobé Hill. They carried with them their lumbering oval oxhide shields, their fighting sticks, and a bundle of spears. Each man wore a charm around his neck. They moved out, chanting a war song, low and musical.

Anta and Maboni watched them go. Then, with Sidalo and his friends, they drove the herds of the Great Place to the back of the neighboring mountains. Word came that Khwane was victorious, and they brought the cattle home.

The army was assembled for the purification. Again there was feasting. The warriors told of the battle. Oba had gathered many men, and they had attacked fiercely. But Khwane had kept his place in the center of the front line until the spears of the enemy looked like thorns in his oxhide shield. Oba had always avoided long battles. Dismayed by his losses, he turned away. His warriors retreated in disorder.

That evening, in the sleeping hut, Diko said, "*Éwe*, truly, Oba's men were no better than an army of children."

"What was it like?" Anta asked.

"When I saw the spears coming toward me, I sidestepped them," Diko boasted. "And when my own were used up, I picked up and returned those thrown by the enemy. But you are too young to think of such things."

chapter 2

Overnight, the rhythm of life at the Great Place changed. A violent thunderstorm struck the hills, and as the rains poured down and the streams and rivulets swelled, the thoughts of the women turned to the work that lay ahead. The time for planting crops had come. The boys would take the cattle higher for the lush grasses.

At early dawn they went up with the herds, some hundreds in number, and returned as the sun was setting behind the hills. Anta saw the wives of the Great Place sowing the fields, throwing the seed in all directions. Later, when the endless task of weeding began, he saw them shoulder their hoes and make for the vegetable lands. There, standing in a line, they would chant their songs, bodies moving rhythmically while they plied their hoes throughout the long hours of the morning. All work is better in company. A woman must be a good neighbor, they sang. Often he passed them in the young wife's field, the field of Tandeka. And the little path that they tracked through the grass was called Tandeka's path. They knew she would help each of them in turn, for there was always a field that needed planting or weeding.

On his way to the cattle fold in the mornings Anta would walk by Tandeka's hut in the hope that she would come out with a handful of corn kernels for him. He would tuck them away in his blanket and share them later with the herd boys. He did not mind Diko's teasing remarks, except for one: that Balakazi, his mother, had been displeased when their father had taken Tandeka as his wife without consulting her. Of course, thought Anta, Diko was only repeating what he had heard his own mother say. It was hard to think that anyone would not like Tandeka, who was so friendly. And everyone said she was beautiful, with a voice like the song of a *mlonji* on the wing.

One day, while they were out herding, Diko brought their father's favorite bull, known for his fighting qualities, to feed on the same path as another bull of renown. Anta was amazed that he would do it. The two bulls roared and stamped, pawing the ground with their forehooves, kicking up dust and earth into the air.

Then, heads down, they locked horns and started to fight. With a sense of wrongdoing Anta watched with the boys, terrified, as Diko shouted out challenges to the bulls. "It is the washing of the horns!" Diko yelled, whipping up their excitement.

"The washing of the horns!" they all cried after him.

The horns of one of the bulls were about to be

washed in the blood of the other. Fortunately the animals separated, but later, at home, when it was found that Khwane's bull had been injured, Diko denied having anything to do with it. "I saw them fighting from afar," he said to their father, knowing that the boys would never tell.

Sometimes in the pastures Anta and Maboni tried to ride one of the calves. When they were little, they used to race the goats. Staying on the back of a calf was not as easy as it seemed. Anta learned to grab hold of the loose skin around the calf's neck and shoulders and to keep his legs tight against its body. Afterwards, when the calf began to respond only to him, his father knew that he had been riding it but said nothing.

There was a certain pool where they liked to go. Each day, after stripping off their bits of blanket, they splashed, dived, and swam in the deepest parts. Once, as they were leaning over and looking at their own reflections in the water, Anta was startled to see the image of Diko, who had suddenly come up behind him. After swimming they usually formed hunting parties, each one with his bundle of sticks beating the reeds around the pool for small birds and field mice. They roasted their game over a dung fire, and Sidalo made sure that they shared fairly. To one boy he gave the head of a mouse, to another a foreleg or a hind leg, still sizzling and juicy.

One afternoon, when they were on their way to the pool again, Maboni told them not to go there anymore. "Why not?" they asked him.

"Someone is putting medicines there to harm us," he said.

"Why to harm us?" they wanted to know.

"I cannot tell you why, but I know. I can see it," he answered. So solemn was his voice, so strange were his eyes that no one, not even Diko, went there again.

That evening, after milking time, a messenger arrived at the Great Place with news of a raid on an outlying fold. The men of the place had tracked the cattle, he said, turning back only when it was clear that their animals had been driven over the mountain pass leading to Oba's country. They were asking their chief's permission to go after them.

Why would Oba risk war so soon after defeat and over little more than a hundred head? Anta wondered. Perhaps the raid had been carried out without his consent, Diko suggested. As the days went by, the raids grew more frequent, and Oba's men more daring. "Why does our father not stop them?" Anta asked over and over. Each new incident aroused his longing to be old enough for raids and battles. "Next time I shall go too," he stated.

"You are not a man," said Diko. And he began to talk about their father's wives.

Diko was always repeating things he heard in his

mother's hut. Yesterday, said he, the great wife had invited the wives to go with her to the forest and gather firewood. When they arrived there, the women separated. After a while his mother, Thubisi, came upon Tandeka by chance, and together they sat down to sort out their firewood. Both took care not to build too heavy a load—lest they be thought to have powers and strength that would make others envy them, explained Diko. All at once a honey bird fluttered down out of a tree and, flying toward them, then away again, called them to follow. Dropping everything, they set off after the little bird, whose urgent calls guided them to a bees' nest. After gathering the honeycomb and leaving a piece on the ground for the bird, they returned to the place where they had left their bundles of wood. There they sat and ate the honeycomb. According to Thubisi, Tandeka saw that for every piece of honeycomb she was eating, she was saving another piece, but it was only when she wrapped up what she had laid aside that Tandeka asked her why she had not told her to put some aside too. And Thubisi had answered, "A married woman knows to put something aside." Last night, Diko went on, when their father stopped by to give instructions about the cattle, his mother had served him a piece of honeycomb on a clay plate.

Anta did not know what to make of the story. Tandeka had been wrong not to think of her husband, and he might well punish her. But why did Thubisi not tell her? Was it not the duty of a senior wife to teach a young wife how to behave?

By morning all the wives knew that Khwane had found out about the honeycomb, yet he had not been angry with Tandeka when he had visited her in her hut last night. It confirmed what they were saying among themselves. He was favoring his youngest wife; he had become blinded by her beauty. "She has honey on her tongue but brings none to the home," Thubisi mumbled under her breath. The wives said nothing to Tandeka and were careful not to show their feelings in the presence of their husband.

But Thubisi soon grew bolder and found an opportunity to complain to Khwane. "Your little wife did not cook food for Diko, the eldest son of the house," she told him.

On another occasion, when Khwane praised his wives for the excellence of his meal, they said, "The young wife did not cook your food well. We had to cook it over again." They thought they could make their husband dislike her or that Tandeka would become so unhappy that she would run away.

The only kind words came from Balakazi, whose duty it was to defend the little wife. The young wives were a nuisance to the older wives, she told herself. Men did not always know how to choose a good wife; that was why she had taken it upon herself to choose Khwane's wives for him. She was silent, however, when Thubisi came to tell her that she had seen Tandeka talking to Nomaliso. With her own ears, said Thubisi, she had heard Tandeka say, "Everyone's heart wishes for a girl."

Anta gave no further thought to the stories about the women until Diko told him that uBhayilam, their father's racing ox, was seen lying outside Tandeka's hut.

"Why was it there?" Anta asked.

"*Éwe*, yes, why?" Diko replied. "The women are saying that Tandeka is working a charm on it.

Other concerns were being forced upon Anta. That evening, as they were driving the cattle home through the mist, Maboni began to complain of pains in his body. The next morning the pains became severe, even to his fingertips, and after a few days he was seized by uncontrollable twitchings. Night after night he had dreams of strange animals that came and spoke to him.

Recognizing the symptoms, his family knew that only an *igqira*, a diviner, could help them. They consulted Gedja, the wise one, she who could reveal the hidden. A woman in her middle years, Gedja was widely respected. She lived on the other side of Nkomkobé Hill. Gedja confirmed that it was the special sickness sent by the ancestors. "He has the white disease," she said. Maboni had received the call to become an *igqira*. "It is the ancestors on his

17

mother's side who are calling him. He is one of us," said Gedja. "The ancestors have messengers. There is a civet cat, which I alone can see, that tells me what to do and gives me power."

The family of Maboni were not sure that they wanted him to be an *igqira*. They would have to let him live with an *igqira* for a year or two, so that he could be taught the art of divining and of making the medicines he would need. The life of an *igqira* is different from that of an ordinary person. He has to be away from his home for long periods, looking for herbs and roots. Moreover, he is not always liked, and sometimes he has many enemies. Maboni's family decided to refuse the call and asked Gedja to treat the boy and lay the spirit. They knew that this might be dangerous for Maboni.

Anta did not set eyes on his friend for several days because Maboni no longer went out with the cattle. There was talk that he was behaving oddly and that he liked to sit alone. When Anta stopped by to see him one afternoon, he found his friend calm in manner and no longer in pain. But when he tried to tell him news of the cattle, he seemed uninterested and strangely detached. Anta walked away bewildered.

Each day, as he went with the herds to the uplands, he noticed the new growth of grasses along the way, patches of tall sweet grass springing up among the sour grass with the summer rain. Water was plentiful, and all was green again.

Now the cattle were let out to graze on the hills close to home. He and the other boys had to watch carefully that the animals did not go too near the places of their neighbors. Herding nearby made it easier to visit Maboni at the end of the day. Most of the time he would find his friend sitting alone some distance from the cattle fold. Once, when Anta asked him why, he replied that he did not like to sit in the midst of many people, for when he was alone, it was easier for him to see what he could not otherwise see.

Late one afternoon Anta left the cattle to continue homeward on their own and went as usual to Maboni's place. His friend had been in pain again, and though he seemed better at times, people thought that his disease must be growing worse because more and more, he showed powers of divining. "He cannot forever remain midway between being a diviner and not being a diviner," they said. Anta was afraid that his friend might die.

He found Maboni standing by the door of his hut, his blanket thrown aside to catch the last warming rays of the sun. Maboni did not greet him. "There is a stranger coming along the path on the other side of the hill," he said. Anta saw that he was looking into the distance as if he had not an inner sight but a sight so clear that he could see from afar the very thing itself. It was becoming known that Maboni could see things that nobody else could see. Anta waited for him to say more, but his friend took no further notice of him.

On his way home he saw that what Maboni had said was true. Approaching along one of the narrow footpaths was a tall young man, his red ochered blanket draped loosely around him. His face was rubbed with clay to protect him from the sun, and from the dust on his body Anta knew that he had journeyed long. "Where do you come from?" Anta asked politely. "Have you had a good journey?" He was impatient to know why he was here but did not want to seem lacking in manners by failing to ask the customary questions. The young man told him that he had come to see the chief. Anta took him to the Great Place.

It was sundown. The cattle had been inspected, and the evening milking had taken place. Along the hedge of the cattle fold the men were sitting about, puffing at their tobacco pipes. Anta lingered with his friends near the gate. Through the dense smoke which was coming out of the doorway of the huts, he could make out the shapes of the women bending over their iron cooking pots. He watched his father enter the reception hut, followed by the stranger. A short time later his father summoned him. He told him that the young man was from one of the cattle posts. They were going there, and he wished Anta to go with them. Anta could not believe it!

From the tales of the older boys a stay at the cattle posts was a happy way of life for several months at a stretch. Each year, in the dry wintertime, large herds were sent to various grazing posts, where the herd boys stayed with them. When the boys returned, they seemed to look taller and stronger, and they knew more about cattle than the others. One could tell which of the boys had been to a cattle post, thought Anta.

There were some posts where none of the boys had been, posts where his father had placed great numbers of cattle in safekeeping. Perhaps they would visit these. In any event, not even Diko or Sidalo had been on a journey with their father.

chapter 3

The next morning Khwane selected the milking cows they would take with them. When they were away from home, milk could be drunk only if they stayed with clansmen, and taking the cows would enable them to keep their sacks of sour milk constantly filled. The very sight of those bulging milk sacks was pleasing to Anta. Clotted sour milk was food for men.

Shortly before sunset Khwane went to the cattle fold to choose a beast for the ancestors. Standing in the middle of the fold beside the wide-horned ox that had been caught and tied, Khwane addressed the ancestral spirits. Speaking to them as man to man, he told them he was going on a journey, and in return for the beast he wanted protection for his family. The first time Anta ever saw such a killing he had been too young to understand why a beast, a thing of value, had to be given. He knew now that it was done not only because the ancestors became hungry but also to keep on good terms with them, for the well-being of the living depended on the goodwill of the dead, the elders of the family who have passed on. He was yet to learn how easily offended and unpredictable they were.

In the early dawn, when the dew was still on the cattle's horns and the cobwebs lay unbroken on the wet, grassy pathways, Khwane and Anta mounted the ride oxen. "Are there no counselors coming with us?" Anta asked.

"No," answered Khwane, but did not say why.

They started out, the hooves of their animals leaving a trail of deep imprints behind them. The tall young man walked ahead, while two herdsmen brought up the rear, driving the milk cows before them. Holding with one hand the reins tied to the nose stick of his ox, Anta looked back, raising his other hand in a farewell greeting to Nomaliso. All the people of the Great Place had gathered to see them go.

Taking one of the grassy tracks that wound down the hill, they crossed the shallow stream below and rode single file along a path through the middle of the cornfields, walled in on either side by the leafy plants towering above them. They were to pass many such fields during the day, rich, fertile lands owned by Khwane. Everywhere they went they saw large numbers of cattle grazing on the plains and in the river valleys, where the grasses were tender and sweet. The air was still. The step of the ride oxen made not a sound in the grass.

They journeyed along narrow trails worn by foot, the numberless paths that crisscrossed the hills, and they stopped for the night at a cluster of huts near the crest of a ridge. When the people saw them coming, they greeted Khwane with the royal salute. Gathering up their blankets with their left hands, they raised their right arms and pointed to the sky, shouting, "You who are Beautiful, you who are Big." Wherever the travelers stopped, they were received with meat and drink, while sleeping mats made of the finest rushes were rolled out for them in the visitor's hut. When they departed in the morning, gifts of cattle were bestowed on Khwane.

They knew they were approaching the first cattle post when they heard a din that shook the air. In the valley below them there was a large herd, and the boys were riding on calves, chasing playfully after the cattle, blowing on oxhorn trumpets, and shouting, making as much noise as they could.

This was a post at which Khwane had placed hundreds of head of cattle in the care of his men. He had done so, he told Anta, because it was less risky than having them all at the Great Place in the event of a raid. Besides, it was wise for a man to try to hide some of his wealth so as not to arouse the envy of those less fortunate. Khwane inspected his herds and, pleased with the increase in numbers, presented a heifer to each of his men.

Every day they visited another cattle post. Their pace began to slow as the course changed from a smooth, even surface to a more rugged terrain. The ride oxen stepped carefully to avoid the holes in the ground made by burrowing animals and the stones that lay almost hidden in the tall grasses. They were in the foothills of the Nunge mountains, and looking back, they could see the green hills they had left behind as well as the tops of the ridges and the groups of huts that lay along them. The slopes ahead were overgrown with bush, and clumps of mimosa spilled into the surrounding ravines. They would have to make their way single file along an old cattle track through the thickets. And here, said their guide, the herdsmen must turn back with the milk cows and the ride oxen and await their return at a cattle post lower down.

Led by their guide, Khwane and Anta continued on foot, shut in by bush so close that not a breath of air found its way through. As bush and scrub gradually gave place to taller trees, they knew they were nearing the forest-clad summit they had seen from the distance. Suddenly they came onto a small plateau hidden by thorn trees. There they spent the night.

When they started out at dawn, the mist hung so low over the summit of the mountain that they could not see the peaks of the ridge above. Below them the ravines lay in darkness. Instead of climbing higher, they descended, creeping on hands and knees where the bush was very dense, scrambling around the large rocks and boulders that had fallen from the cliffs. Anta began to tire. The ravines were forbidding, and he tried not to look at them. His fears grew as their guide took them down a steep bank. After creeping once again through bush and scrub, they entered the silent ravine below.

Great trees reached toward the sky, shutting out the last rays of the afternoon sun. As his eyes became accustomed to the darkness, Anta could make out the small game trails that led through the thick bush. Little streams ran everywhere. On the bank of a river where they rested, he saw heavy tracks crossing endlessly, as if a herd of cattle had been there more than once.

The shadows were deepening into twilight. Now the very stillness frightened him. Were they going to stay all night in the ravine? A fearsome place, and in it lay unseen savage things. An enemy army could hide here, and no one would know. Wild beasts would stalk them in the dark. And this was when the people of the water, the river spirits, roamed.

Single file, Anta in the middle, the three walked on in silence along the riverbank. He did not dare ask where they were going. They had just reached a round clump of brush not far from the place where they had been resting when, without a sound, a small figure stepped out from the shadows and blocked their way. Anta stood rooted to the spot, his whole body numb with fright. The next instant he heard words of greeting in the Khoikhoi tongue. There was a hushed conversation, and then the guide turned away and disappeared into the darkness. They were alone with the stranger.

The little figure led them away from the riverbank, up the side of the ravine, and into what seemed to be a large clearing, where some thorny acacia trees had grown to giant size. Near one of them a low fire was burning. He motioned them to sit down beside it.

Anta stared at the stranger. He was a very old man with a deeply wrinkled face and sharp, alert eyes. Dressed in wildcat skins, the muscles of his arms and legs knotty and thin, he had the look of a man who lived in the open. He was of a race of herders, a people who called themselves Khoikhoi, "men of men." Anta knew about them. He had learned their language from the two at home. It was with Khoikhoi that his father had taken refuge when, as a young counselor, he had quarrelled with Oba. Some of them had become Khwane's followers, returning with him years later and staying on as his most trusted herdsmen after he had been made a chief.

The old man dug some pieces of cooked game from the ashes and invited them to share his food. As Anta sat at the fire trying to keep awake, it seemed to him that something was moving under the trees. He sat bolt upright. Suddenly he caught a familiar odor: the grassy smell of cattle.

Before he could recover from his astonishment, the old man said, "Yes, there are cattle. They know you are here. But let us rest for the night. Tomorrow you will see them."

Anta and his father wrapped themselves tightly in their ochered blankets and lay down beside the fire. The old man used a roll of animal skins to line the shallow sleeping place he had dug in the ground. Anta plied his father with questions.

Years ago, Khwane told him, he had placed a number of cattle in the care of the old Khoikhoi in order to keep them from his enemies. Moving from one pasture to another, the old man had kept the cattle hidden in the ravines, and although the herd had increased tenfold, not a single one had ever been stolen. From time to time he made his whereabouts known to another cattle post. The men there knew he had cattle in his care but had never seen them. Indeed, the cattle knew only their own keeper.

From the outset Khwane had realized that in bringing Anta along, he was placing a great responsibility on the young boy. Although he owned cattle beyond counting, these were precious to him, and he wished no one to know of them, not even his counselors. Usually some accompanied him on his journeys, but he had said that he wished to make this journey without them. He must be sure that the other children would not force Anta to say where he had been. "You will see things here that must remain secret," he told Anta solemnly. "One day all this will be yours." So that was it; they had come to inspect the cattle, Anta thought drowsily. Satisfied, he fell sound asleep.

Khwane had acted on impulse in taking Anta with him. He loved all his children, but this son was closest to his heart. Yet the theft of the cows at the stream showed he had much to learn. Anta's nature was gentle like his own, thought Khwane, but the boy was too trusting, and there was something about him, an immaturity, perhaps a weakness, which needed to be toughened.

At dawn Anta was awakened by the voices of his father and the old one, speaking in the rapid click tongue of the Khoikhoi language. Sitting up, he saw his father stirring the remains of the fire with a stick. The smell of cattle was heavy.

"Now we shall see them," said the old herdsman. "Stay close to me, and do not say a word," he told Anta. With Khwane on one side of the old man, Anta on the other, they walked slowly toward the trees where the herd was still resting. As they came nearer, the old man called out to the cattle and reassured them.

This herd is unaccustomed to strangers, thought Anta. It is dangerous to go closer. He pressed against the old man, gripping his arm tightly. The cattle raised their heads, ears forward, as the old man led Khwane and Anta into the herd. The young bulls became restless and started to rise, but he spoke to them and called them by name. A cow with a newborn calf stood up suddenly. Immediately he reached out and laid his hand on her horn, turning her gently back toward her calf. Anta forgot his fear.

Was it not wondrous? Here they were, walking through this huge herd, surrounded by great bulls and the menacing horns of oxen. The place itself was so still, so hidden, like no place he had ever known. Even the cattle were different. Their eyes followed every movement of the old man. They were as alert as wild things ready to run or to spring.

As they moved among the cattle, he could see how pleased his father was. The cattle were fat and sleek, and there were many young calves. Soon, however, Khwane made a sign. The old man gave a loud whistle, drew breath, and then whistled again. A few moments later a huge black-and-white bull came toward them through the herd. The old man held out his hand, and the bull rubbed his head against it. He scratched the neck and shoulders of the animal and then drew Khwane and Anta closer. They held themselves very still as the bull snorted and sniffed at their bodies with his wet nose. "He has taken your scent," said the old man. "You will be safe with the herd." Then he led them back to the fire.

"That was the leader of the herd," Khwane explained. "But do not be deceived," he told Anta. "Had the old one not been with us, we would have been killed."

The old herdsman took several strips of dried antelope meat from a skin bag. After they had eaten, he tied the bag firmly to his side with thongs of hide and strapped his roll of animal skins flat against his back. He showed Anta how to fold his blanket and how to fasten it around his waist. "We will need to move freely," he said.

"Then you are coming with us?" asked Anta. "But who will be with the cattle?"

The old man smiled. "They are coming too."

When they were ready, he put his fingers to his mouth and whistled sharply three times. While they watched, the leader bull circled the herd, and the groups of cattle rose as he passed them. The old man turned away and led Khwane and Anta out of the clearing. When Anta glanced back, he saw the cattle standing silently.

And now it came to him that his father was carrying out some plan. He was telling the old herder that the mountain pass was much too narrow, the rocks on each side nearly touching the other. Once they were out of the ravines, said his father, he would show him the way.

Just beyond the clearing the old man paused, and pursing his lips, he gave the slow, falling call of the red-eyed dove. The *umakhulu*, thought Anta, and so perfectly. Only someone living in the wilderness could do it. But why? After crossing the river, the three pushed on through underbrush and along game trails, avoiding tree stumps and hook thorn. The old man stopped often, giving again the plain-

31

tive call. When they were clambering up the steep side of the ravine, grabbing hold of vines and creepers, Anta looked down. Below him the ravine was filled with cattle, spread so thickly among the bushes that it seemed as if the scrub were alive. The herd was following them.

They halted when they reached the head of the ravine and rested under the dense, spreading branches of a wild fig. Then, with the old man still cooing and chirring to the cattle, they slowly climbed down into yet another ravine. When they had crossed it and scaled its bush-covered side, they were on high, open ground. Anta saw that the fingerlike spurs of the mountain were behind them, and at last he understood. They had been making a big circle uphill through the ravines in order to reach the back of the mountain. Now, they saw in front of them a flat-topped plateau surrounded by peaks and rough stony ridges, the site of Oba's Great Place. They had approached it from behind, the secret way which Oba had once revealed to a few trusted counselors. He felt secure from attack because his Great Place was ringed by mountains.

Hidden behind a boulder, the three looked out onto the plateau across the ravine. Grouped in a half circle around the royal cattle folds, their doors facing eastward, were Oba's mud-walled huts. The large courtyard was filled with warriors, who were feasting and dancing. Puffs of smoke rose from the cooking pots outside the huts. The army was preparing for battle.

He had expected this, said Khwane, because he had sent his spies into Oba's country to steal the headpieces of his warriors, the blue crane plumes stored in a hut with the weapons. Anta knew that this was not only an insult to the warriors who had earned them but a challenge to Oba himself. The blue crane feathers belonged to a chief to give as he pleased, and an attack on his property was a hostile act against him. It had been an open invitation to war.

The sun went down, and dusk came swiftly. As night fell, they heard the chant of hundreds of voices singing their war songs. The old herdsman looked at Khwane, who nodded. The old man put two fingers into his mouth and made the mournful, throaty noise of an owl, once, twice, and then again. Anta's blood ran cold. The calling owls caused fear in his own people, and even to imitate an owl was dangerous.

There was a rumble along the slopes, a low, rolling sound like distant thunder. The old man listened intently. The sound grew louder. "Let us go," he said suddenly. Anta could hear the lowing of cattle. The three hurriedly crossed the shallow ravine and started up the bushy side to Oba's Great Place. Now and then the old man stopped and repeated the owl cry. When they reached the top of the ridge, they ran to take cover behind the great loose stones that lay at the edge of the summit. Once again the old man brought his fingers to his mouth and gave two long, loud hoots. Anta saw the dark shapes of the cattle as they came over the rim, veered to the right, and poured down toward the cattle folds.

Alarmed by the sound of thunder, the warriors had thought that a storm was approaching. But those who heard the calls of the owl drawing closer trembled at the omen that came on the eve of battle. The next they knew, a pounding of hooves shattered the night. The cattle, in their terrible charge, smashed through the royal folds and, bellowing fiercely, horns clashing, swept with them hundreds of beasts from Oba's herd as they stampeded into the bed of the ravine. As suddenly as it had begun, it was over.

Khwane, Anta, and the old man hid in the ravine until morning. "Oba will suspect that it was my cattle. He will think I have strong medicines. He will believe that my herds can be made to attack wherever I please," Khwane told Anta. "I have humiliated him in front of his people and all his warriors. He will stay away now. His horns are broken."

With the first light they rounded up the cattle, their own and those they had captured, and returned to the old man's hidden place. There they separated the animals and then took Oba's herd to the cattle post lower down. Khwane's men were excited to see their chief bring cattle and did not question it. They were accustomed to receiving booty without ever caring to know where it came from.

At the Great Place, some days later, two pairs of brindled oxen arrived for Khwane, along with a message from Oba: "I am your brother." Knowing nothing of what had gone before, Khwane's counselors were astonished. Even Oba must know the greatness of their chief, Khwane, son of Vukuthu, they said. Khwane's reputation grew among the neighboring peoples who frequently in the past had plundered his cattle folds. And peace came to his country.

chapter 4

Anta's life took on its old routine, the going out with the cattle and the returning at night. He longed to boast about the extraordinary things he had seen and done but did not betray his father's trust. Shy by nature, he began to change, and like all the other fifteen-year-olds, he now seemed to have not a care in the world. He and his friends became wild and lawless. They showed no respect for the property of others. Whenever they could, they pilfered food and tobacco from the family huts, and though they took care not to be caught, they knew that their petty thefts would be shrugged off as boyish mischief. They were not yet men. No one expected them to behave otherwise.

For Anta this was a time of happy abandon. Mindless of those around him, he scarcely noticed that the once-cheerful Tandeka had grown sad and withdrawn. Formerly, at the close of the day, before it was time to prepare the evening meal, the wives would call to her as they passed her hut, inviting her to join them in a visit to a neighbor. They would sit in a circle, exchanging gossip and smoking their pipes. Sometimes Tandeka had taken along one of her calabashes to trade with the women for other utensils, and in the good-natured wrangling that went on, she had been their equal. But now she no longer joined them. She spent every moment she could tending the tobacco and gourds that grew near her cooking hut or weeding the cornfields that lay within walking distance of her home. Once, when she stayed in her hut, the women shouted, "Come out, come out of the darkness. It is not good to sit alone." Among themselves they spoke differently. "She is proud. She does not look at people when she greets them," they said. "She is not a good neighbor. She does not brew."

"She is the cow that grazes alone," Thubisi said quietly.

Tandeka could think of one thing only. A woman needed daughters to help her work in the fields, grind corn, and keep the mud floors and walls of her hut freshly smeared. Boys were necessary, of course, because the line of a woman's house is carried on through her sons, and it is the sons who will look after her when she grows old. But boys were mere things, persons of no sense, and they would remain so until they became men. A girl like Nomaliso had been helping her mother from the time she had barely learned to walk. Balakazi, the great wife, liked to boast that when Nomaliso was ten, she was already able to run a household. Nomaliso came often to Tandeka's home and took care of her two young sons while she was in the fields. Not so long ago she used to imitate the women, balancing a small calabash of water on her head. Soon she would be earning bridewealth for her mother's house. Girls are the cattle of the family, Tandeka brooded. She might lose her husband's affections if he had to give cattle from his own herd when her sons became old enough to marry. The wives scorned her, and without daughters she would never gain standing among them.

It was not in vain that Tandeka tended her gardens. By thinning the crowded seedlings, she had ensured their healthy growth, and after months of careful weeding her fields showed promise of unusual abundance. The beans and melons were beginning to ripen; the corn had grown to a height taller than her head, the pale green leaves curling gracefully at the edges. Each stalk was strong and vigorous and swollen on the side where the young cobs had begun to form. And underneath these leafy stalks, trailing over the ground in every direction, the pumpkins were bearing fruit.

When they should have been mindful of the cattle that might stray into the gardens, the older boys were indulging in stick fights, their favorite pastime. More and more Anta took part. Since he was five years old, he had carried a stick, and often, as he and Maboni walked along, one of them would stop and immediately they would begin to spar with their sticks. Even at three, when his mother would pretend to hit him, he knew how to put up one arm to defend himself and would try to hit back. A boy was never without a stick.

One afternoon in the fields Diko arranged a contest in stick fighting and made the boys pair off for single combat. Sidalo noticed that Anta's opponent was a seventeen-year-old boy from a neighboring ridge, and he wondered why Diko was forcing him to fight someone bigger and stronger. But Diko, the eldest, had to be obeyed, or else he was likely to beat up Anta. Sidalo decided to keep an eye on his younger half brother.

As the boys threw aside their blankets and prepared for the match, Sidalo helped Anta wrap a small cloth around his hand and the end of the fighting stick, in order to protect him from a blow that might disable him. This long fighting stick, pointed at the tip, was his principal weapon, but in his left hand he carried an even more dangerous one, a short, knobbed stick, which he held by the middle.

The boys started off in playful mood. Sidalo saw that Anta was neatly turning aside his opponent's blows and striking back with a few of his own. He hits like a horn, Sidalo thought proudly. But suddenly the other boy was hitting harder with his long stick. When he raised his left arm as if to bring down the short stick on Anta's head, Sidalo rushed to his half brother's defense. With a powerful blow he knocked the knobbed stick from the boy's hand. Facing each other angrily, the two began to fight in earnest, lunging and striking with their long sticks. Now Diko became alarmed. He yelled to them both to stop. The fight broke up, and the other boy walked off to collect his oxen.

The next morning a group of older boys appeared in the fields and sat down, waiting for Diko to approach them. They had come to avenge the honor of their kinsman. After an exchange of taunts and threats a time was set for the battle between the herd boys of the two neighboring ridges.

That afternoon the boys prepared themselves. Anta was excited at the prospect of his first big stick fight. Stripped for action like the others, he wore only a small ochered blanket around his loincloth, while Diko and his friends put on leggings hung with dry cocoons, filled with pebbles to make them rattle. Each one wrapped a torn piece of blanket around his parrying hand. Each was ready to test his own strength in a really good fight.

Diko and his group made their way to the fighting ground. Nomaliso and the other girls came behind them. Their short goatskin skirts were burnished and bright. Soon the boys from the neighboring ridge arrived, followed by some girls. The two groups of boys paraded, waved their sticks, and yelled their battle cries. Then, with wild jumps and stamps, they danced to the singing and handclapping of the girls.

On the slopes of the two ridges, a crowd of women had gathered, shouting and jeering at one another. Word soon reached Khwane that a stick fight was about to take place. Stick fights, he knew, meant cracked skulls and bloodshed and usually ended by involving the men. He ordered his counselors to put a stop to it at once. "Boys settle things by the stick," he said angrily; "men must settle them by words." As the sounds of the dance died down, just moments before the onset of battle, two of Khwane's counselors arrived and ordered the boys to disperse.

"He must be sent into the hills," said Khwane to his counselors. He was talking of Anta, whose behavior of late had come to his attention. Only the other day he had forceably taken from a woman the melons she was carrying on her return from the fields. Anta had become rowdy, slovenly in his appearance, and rude to the women. It would sober the boy to undergo the rites, Khwane said.

But his counselors criticized him for wanting to send Anta off when he was not even fully sixteen. "The chief is doing a bad thing," they mumbled. "A boy must grow to the required age."

Not wanting to offend them, Khwane explained that he had good reason for his decision. "He is influenced by older boys," he said. "He must go before he becomes so unruly that he cannot be disciplined."

Khwane knew that it was Diko who was to blame

for the stick fight, and it was clear to him that he was challenging Anta. He felt a responsibility for Diko, as he did for all his children. Diko had courage and daring, but he was hotheaded. His age, strength, and leadership made him an aggressive rival for succession. Anta would have to learn to contend with that. But now he must start growing up.

Anta was bewildered when one of his father's men came in the early morning and led him from his hut. After a few more boys had been rounded up, he realized what was happening. He, the chief's son, was being sent away, and so others would go also. Later, when he was a chief, they could say that they had become men with Anta. The family of Maboni decided that he should wait.

This was the day which all the boys dreaded. To prepare them for the rites, their heads were shaved, and each was given a new white blanket, a new knobbed stick, and a sharp spear. In the evening a goat was killed and cooked for Anta, and he had to sit in the cattle fold and eat the meat from the animal's right foreleg before the members of the family could eat the rest. Diko said that this was to prevent a boy from dying or going mad during the rites.

Anta wished he could run away. However, at dawn the following day, as they were being taken down to the river to wash off the things of their past, he saw that they were surrounded by several men carrying knobbed sticks, who seemed to be ready for anyone who might try just that. The ordeal of circumcision was to begin.

After bathing, they were led into the fields, and near a little straw hut which had been built for them, naked, shivering with cold and fright, they sat down in the company of men of the neighborhood and waited for Mlandu, who would perform the rite. At sunrise they heard him come, for as he strode past the family huts, the women set up an incessant wail, trilling with their tongues, and ending with a sudden, terrifying shriek. The boys stood up as Mlandu arrived. He came to Anta first. Sick with fear, Anta knew that he must not cry out. He felt the burning pain from Mlandu's knife, and he heard Mlandu say, "You are a man!"

"I am a man!" he recited as Mlandu passed to the next in line.

Rubbed with white clay from head to foot, Anta and the others wrapped themselves in their new blankets and listened silently as old Namba told them how they must behave. Then they were marched off to their new grass hut where they would stay, separated from their past and their everyday life.

For three months they endured the hardships that would strengthen them and prepare them for manhood. Under the stict care of old Namba they drank nothing but water muddied with antheap and ate food made unsavory, such as meat that was roasted over a fire of bitter leaves. They bathed in cold streams and received frequent beatings, even if they did not break a single rule. Every day they practiced the ceremonial dance, wearing short, stiff reed skirts and towering headdresses.

Anta was overwhelmed by the strangeness of what was taking place. His friends were so sober they hardly spoke to one another. Everything was unfamiliar. These were the boys he had known always, but now there was no jesting, no rough play. At the dances he could not recognize them. Keening, swaying, bending, their faces hidden under the tall reed masks, they were like creatures he had never seen before. It was all mysterious and frightening. So much of what they did he could not understand, but he knew his life had changed; boyhood was gone.

Then it was time for the coming-out rites. In single file they walked to the river, where they washed away the white clay on their bodies. At the little hut they draped themselves head to foot in their new white blankets, and leaving the garments and utensils used by them during their stay, they walked away, in single file again, forbidden to look back as the thatched hut was set alight and burst into flames behind them.

At home they were received with feasting and celebration. They gathered at the cattle fold. First old

Namba and then each of the elders reminded them of their new duties: Now that they were men, they must behave as men and live in a way that was pleasing to the ancestors. They must have dignity, show respect for women and other men, and provide for their parents as long as they lived. For the next three months they must walk very slowly and speak only in low voices. To do otherwise would be boastful.

As they sat in the hot sun, the old men rambling on, Anta's thoughts drifted. It seemed so long ago: First he had been allowed to take out the calves from their hut at milking time; then he had herded the calves; at last he had herded not only the calves and the goats but all the cattle. And at last he had grown to be a man. Suddenly he heard his father's voice. "You have attained manhood," said Khwane to Anta, "but you are merely a new man."

About the rest of their homecoming Anta afterwards remembered only one thing: He and the other new men were sitting in a row next to the cattle fold while the guests filed past, bringing gifts, a pumpkin or some gourds, a fowl or a goat, when all at once his father came from the pen, driving before him a strong young ox. It was his gift to Anta.

Unbelieving, Anta marveled at the beauty of the young ox. Its pendent horns curved gracefully along each side of its jaws. It had stipples of black and white everywhere and black forelegs, black-and-white stipples, the color favored by the ancestors. As he stroked the smooth head, Anta saw himself wandering in the forest with his own ox. "Hlatikulu, Big Forest," he addressed the ox. The name had come to his mind instantly. Raising his head, the animal bellowed in response. And joyously Anta chanted, "Bellow, oh beautiful ox with the curving horn, you and I will sing together." Of course, it was still his father's ox because until the day he married, it would be among his father's herd, but in his heart the beast was his alone.

chapter 5

All of Anta's thoughts and attentions were now centered on Big Forest. The very next day he began training him to respond to the sound of his voice; without touching him, he talked to his ox, calling to him by name, not loudly but in a deep and quiet tone, the way the men spoke to the cattle.

He had once seen a man become impatient with his ox when it came out of the fold too slowly. Instead of talking to the beast, he struck it. Afterwards he said that he must have been bewitched to have lost his temper with his ox. At the time the animal had turned its head to look at him, and later, when the rest of the herd was grazing, it had refused to graze. And once, when Diko had failed to shut the gate of the cattle fold securely, his father had lashed out at him with his whip, but instead of hitting Diko, he hit the legs of one of the oxen. That same day the ox took revenge by suddenly rushing at his father and trying to gore him. An ox knew when it was being well treated, thought Anta.

In the pasture, through sheer happiness, he burst into song, praising his ox for its gentleness and beauty. "Beast that attracts every eye as you graze in

the field, you are proud, proud of your horns,"
he chanted. And on the way home he mimed its
gait, holding his arms in the shape of the animal's
horns.

His friends laughed with delight when he leaped
and danced behind his ox, calling out its name and
the name of the clan. "Look, look at his ox with the
black-and-white blanket, girded with leggings," they
sang.

When they reached home, Tandeka was standing
in the small vegetable garden beside her cooking
hut. She was wearing a long cowhide skirt, a black
turban as usual, and necklaces and armbands of little blue beads. The sun turned the color of her
ochered garments deep red. As Anta walked past
her hut, Tandeka stopped him and gave him some
corncobs which she had saved for his ox. In her lilt-
ing voice she admired Big Forest, saying, "You have
the best ox of all. For yours is an ox with a speckled
face." Pleased by her praise, Anta stood and talked
with her for a while.

Thubisi saw this and immediately told the others,
"She is feeding his ox."

After sunset, when all the cattle had been penned,
Khwane allowed the older boys to take a few of the
oxen out for a practice race. Anta asked his father's
permission to let Big Forest run. He watched him
eagerly, boasting that he would train his ox to be so
fast that one day he could use him for running down

antelope. When he returned, he found Maboni standing near the cattle fold, staring off toward the hills. With that strange light in his eyes Maboni turned toward him, and speaking in a voice somewhat different from his normal one, he said, "This ox will lead you into danger." The words sent a chill through Anta.

In the days that followed, while the corn was ripening, the women and children watched for the appearance of the harvest bird. Soon it would be time for Khwane to taste the first grains; then he would allow them to bring in their crops.

Returning early one day to mend the brushwood gate, Anta took a small path through his mother's cornfield, surprising Nomaliso and her friends as they emerged from the dense forest of stalks. By their guilty looks he knew at once that they had been eating the green corn. He himself had done this many a time, although it was forbidden before the ceremony of the new foods. Without letting on that he knew what they were up to, he chatted with them and went on his way.

As he stepped into the open at the edge of the cornfield, he saw his father's wives walking single file in the direction of Tandeka's gardens. Yesterday, when he had helped Tandeka with the repair of her hut, she had told him she was going off early to cut thatch grass for the roof, and since this grew in a place far down the valley, he knew she would be gone all day. His curiosity was aroused. Why in her absence were his father's wives entering her land?

He followed the women into the field and caught up with them when they stopped on the little footpath between the rows of corn. Hiding among the plants, he saw them draw together and stand in a group, looking at the sheaves of leafy wrappings protecting the well-formed cobs. He was so close to them he could hear their conversation.

"Why is it," said Thubisi, "that hers is the only garden bearing good food this year? In all the other fields the stalks are lean and dry and the heads are small. But in hers the plants stand tall and heavy. The cornstalk is carrying its cob as the mother carries her child on her back."

"It is said that she burned medicines in the corners of her field, and the smoke was seen to blow across our lands," said another wife. "Has she used her medicines against us? Has she used medicines stronger than our own?"

Anta wished his mother would defend Tandeka, but she said nothing. She let the others talk. Tandeka's ways were secretive, the wives continued. She had refused to join their circle in an exchange of news. What does one say of a person who has no news? She must be one who loves darkness rather than light, the sort of person who sits alone and eats her food alone, begrudging others. Then can she be expected to share her good fortune? When the new corn was garnered, would she not hide her wealth from them?

As the women turned to go, Thubisi said, in a voice so quiet that Anta could scarcely hear, "She who sits alone plots evil."

chapter 6

From the great hut the next day came word that Nomaliso was ill. All morning she lay on her reed mat covered with blankets, complaining of pains in her head, limbs, and abdomen. Balakazi hovered over her, giving her a brew made from herbs which she always kept in her hut. She knew how to treat fevers, but this was more than fever, she told herself. By midday she could no longer hide her uneasiness. It was strange that only Nomaliso had fallen ill while all the other children were well. She sent a message with one of the older girls to inform Khwane.

"Go and tell those who belong to the hearth," she ordered another. Everyone must be told, for in times of trouble the sickness of one was the concern of all. As the news reached the rest of the family, the mothers hurried over to the great hut, and in low voices they talked about Nomaliso. Perhaps someone had buried poison near the threshold and had spoken Nomaliso's name so that only she, walking over it, would be affected.

When Khwane arrived, he addressed the sick girl. "Did you not see something in your sleep?" he asked.

"Yes," she replied, "for two nights I have seen the red-and-white ox with the winglike horns."

"Then that is the beast which the ancestors want," said Khwane. He would give them the ox which they had demanded in Nomaliso's dream. There was no need to call an *igqira* to interpret it.

At sunset, having summoned all the members of his family to attend, Khwane entered the cattle fold. A few of the men stripped off their ochered blankets and followed him. Outside the gate the women sat in a circle, silent for once, while Anta and his friends leaned on their knobbed sticks, waiting expectantly. The atmosphere was tense. This was the time of day when the spirits of the dead were closest to their living kin.

As Khwane stood in the middle of the fold, holding in his right hand the spear used for a killing, the herd sensed trouble and began to mill uneasily. Pressing close against the hedge, the cattle circled around him in the dust, butting one another, the sound of their hoofbeats sharp and urgent on the hard ground. The red-and-white ox seemed particularly frightened. It was pushing its way to the gate, trying to escape, when Khwane gave the order that it be caught. Standing beside the ox, which lay on its right side in the middle of the fold, hind legs trussed, its head pointing to the gateway, Khwane faced east and spoke to the ancestors. "Come, spirits of the house of Vukuthu. If you are hungry, here is meat." His voice became reproachful as he told them that next time they must come openly to ask for food without bringing sickness. Then he praised them, recounting the brave deeds they had done while living, and called upon them to let Nomaliso get well.

Before he could proceed with the kill, he had to make the ox bellow to call the ancestor spirits. If the ox did not do so, he would not kill it because this would be a sign that the offering was not acceptable. Bending down beside the ox, he gave it a stab in the belly with his spear. It was then that the unexpected happened. Instead of bellowing, the ox uttered only a short, half-stifled groan and died. There was a silence, strange and ominous, followed by the sound of anxiouis snorts from the herd, unnerved by the smell of blood. Alarmed, the men and women neither looked at one another nor spoke. What could be the meaning of the sudden death of the ox? Was it a warning from the ancestors? Would Nomaliso die?

Recovering his composure, Khwane spoke. "The spirits do not want it. I do not know why." Perhaps they wanted a white goat before the sacrifice of the ox, he thought; perhaps it was the wrong ox, or perhaps the ancestors had not sent the illness. "I shall ask a diviner to find out what the spirits wanted, and I shall give them a second ox to make up for the beast that did not bellow. Meanwhile, let Hlubi be called." His voice was loud and firm. For the sake of his kinsmen he controlled his fears, but inwardly he dreaded the anger of the ancestors.

On their return to Balakazi's hut the wives praised their husband for his decision. Word would be sent to Hlubi in the morning. Indeed, it was time to send for an *ixhwele*, a man of medicine, rather than wait until the disease had grown too powerful. There was no *ixhwele* better than Hlubi, they agreed. He could cure a person of anything except an illness sent by the ancestors, and no *ixhwele* can do that.

Hlubi had inherited his knowledge of healing plants from his father, a master, a bull among *ixhwele*. From him he had learned the powers of all the herbs and how to use them. Hlubi's reputation had spread far and wide. He had been living among the Yalo people some distance to the north, but Khwane had lured him away with gifts. Now he lived just beyond Nkomkobé Hill, rich in the herds that his skills had earned for him.

With the approach of this year's harvest Khwane had asked Hlubi to protect the vegetable gardens from thieves, and at dawn that very morning he had buried strong medicines among the crops so that a thief would be transfixed to the spot, unable to move until the owner arrived. He was returning from the fields when he was met by a worried-looking Anta, who brought him the news of Nomaliso's illness. He was to come to the great hut at once. But Hlubi needed time to dig the roots and gather the fresh herbs with which to treat his patient. Several hours later he arrived at the Great Place. Without hurrying, he squatted on the ground inside the hut and undid the calabashes and horns of medicine tied around his body. After mixing dried bulbs and the husks of wild fruit, he put them in a clay pot of water over the fire and instructed Balakazi to see to it that the sick girl inhaled the smoke. Without looking at Nomaliso, he departed, saying he would come the next day.

In the morning Balakazi was waiting for him at the door of the hut. "It must be more than fever," she told Hlubi the moment he arrived.

"We will know soon," he replied, glancing at Nomaliso, who lay motionless on her mat, breathing rapidly, her eyes white with terror. He ordered that damp cow dung be brought from the cattle fold. Balakazi accompanied one of the children and, forbidden by custom to enter the fold, stood outside the hedge, pointing out which patches of cow dung were to be collected. Using it as a poultice, Hlubi applied it to Nomaliso's stomach and kneaded thick plasters of dung to her arms and neck as well. By this time the hut was crowded with all the members of the family, Anta pushing to the front of the silent onlookers. After working the poultice with his hands for some time, Hlubi plunged one hand into it and held up a pinch of dung. He rinsed it in water, extracted something from it with his other hand, and, holding it up to Nomaliso and the others, declared that he had found the cause of her illness. "It was a bewitchment," he announced triumphantly.

No one approached to examine what he had discovered. Knowing it to be the thing which had been used against Nomaliso, they gave it a frightened glance and looked away. "She will now get well," said Hlubi, and he departed, leaving behind some roots for her to chew. His reassurance about her recovery had an immediate effect on Nomaliso. Her body relaxed, her breathing became normal, and her eyes grew calm.

As Hlubi left the great hut, the mothers gathered around Balakazi in earnest consultation. It was not enough that Nomaliso had been cured, they said; it was necessary to find out who had bewitched her. Since the ancestors had not sent the sickness, where had it come from? They would ask their husband, Khwane, for permission to inquire of a witchfinder. There were several who lived nearby, but it is better to consult someone farther away, one who does not hear the talk. They would seek out Gedja, the wise one. She was a diviner to be feared because of her great power to smell out an enemy.

Early the next morning Anta saw a solemn procession of all his father's wives and relatives start out from the Great Place, and he could tell that they were on their way to a witchfinder. Silent, unsmiling, carrying long sticks in their hands, they walked past him single file through the yellow grass. He did not try to join them because he knew that no one of his age would be allowed there.

When the men and women reached Gedja's place, they sat down in a circle outside her hut, leaving space to admit Gedja and her attendants, and without announcing their presence, they waited quietly for her to appear.

Suddenly Gedja rushed out and sprang into the circle. Dressed in white beads and white goatskins, one side of her face rubbed with white clay, the other with charcoal, furs and feathers tied around her waist, she jumped and danced in a frantic manner, waving a stick with a white cow's tail tied on the end. Eagerly the people watched every movement of her body. As she contorted herself and gesticulated wildly, the men beat their sticks on rolls of cowhide, while the women clapped their hands and chanted their songs. Faster and faster went the rhythm. Breathless, the sweat pouring down her, Gedja continued her jolting and stamping dance. So great was the dust which rose under her feet that everyone started to cough.

Ceasing abruptly, Gedja retired to where her attendants sat. She did not ask the people the reason for their visit, nor did they say why they had come. If she could not tell them this, how could she seek out an evildoer? They waited in silence.

Gedja began with the statement that they had come on an important matter, to which assented, clapping their hands loudly and speaking out firmly.

"Siyavuma, we agree," they said, because it was true.

"You have come about a beast," said Gedja.

"Siyavuma, we agree," they replied, but by their tone of indifference and their halfhearted clapping she could tell that the matter had nothing to do with cattle. She had not been in earnest, she hastened to assure them, it was something that was lost.

"We do not hear," said the people calmly.

Trying again, Gedja said, "You have come about a man."

"Siyavuma, we agree." Their clapping was short and unenthusiastic.

"It is about a boy."

"Siyavuma," they answered coldly.

"No, it is about a girl." This time the response was strong, the clapping vigorous.

"A sick girl."

"Siyavuma," the people roared.

"The girl is getting well. It was a bewitch ment."

"Siyavuma," they shouted, clapping excitedly. She had established the point. Now she would have to tell them who had caused it.

Like a man who has lost his cattle and then, finding a track, returns again and again to it, Gedja led them along step by step. Her piercing eyes seemed to look right through them as she watched their faces, reading from it one truth after another. They agreed with her every statement, disputing nothing, for they had come to ask of one who knows.

"Someone has ill-wished her," Gedja said.

"Siyavuma, siyavuma."

"Someone who has reason for jealousy."

"Siyavuma," they cried.

Alert to their every response, Gedja hinted at various relatives and members of the home among whom there was likely to be hostility. Then she announced, "It is a woman, a wife of an important man, not a daughter, not a great wife." Pausing only to note the effect of her words, Gedja went on. "She is a woman who has borne sons but not daughters. Her own people will deny that she is guilty. They will ask to be shown that which she used for her witchcraft. But it cannot all be shown. The poison is in her heart!"

A shocked silence followed Gedja's words. Without mentioning names, she had told them what they wanted to hear. It was indeed as they had known all along; only now it was confirmed by one gifted with special powers. Balakazi, the great wife, rose to her feet and moved quietly away from Tandeka. One by one the others rose and followed Balakazi. Now they understood the meaning of the sudden death of the ox. It was a warning from the ancestors that evil was afoot. She had wanted to kill Nomaliso, her own kin. Khwane would have to be told that his youngest wife was a witch.

Shunned by all, Tandeka sat, dazed by the terrible announcement. She wanted to cry out that she had done nothing, but there was no one to turn to. She was alone.

The counselors were informed. Thubisi was quick to tell Anta. "Did I not say so? She has death in her pot."

"I will not listen," exclaimed Anta, turning away. "The little mother knows nothing of witchcraft."

When Khwane received the news from the oldest of the counselors, he was angry and refused to believe that Tandeka was guilty of this evil.

"She has bewitched you too," said the counselor. "Otherwise, you would not doubt the word of one whose knowledge comes from the ancestors." Months ago, when he had heard the women complain, he had reminded his chief that a man must treat all his wives alike, because if his heart clings to one wife, how can he be loyal to all his kin? Khwane had been risking the wrath of the ancestors. For a man may feel or think what he likes, but the ancestors demand that he behave correctly.

Khwane did not think that he had favored his youngest wife openly. He did his duty, visiting each of his wives in turn and never gave gifts to one wife without giving to all. Balakazi kept order and discipline among them, smoothing over any conflicts and quarrels that arose. They were good wives, and he enjoyed peace and quiet in his home. Other men envied him, saying that he ruled the women as a bull rules the cattle fold. Now there was hate and trouble.

He had seen Tandeka's unhappiness. She longed for daughters. But she was young, and there was time. It did not matter if she never bore him daughters; he had daughters enough. Perhaps she was jealous. Even so, could she ever have done this terrible thing? His heart told him she was kind and good. But Gedja had found her guilty, and the guilty must be punished. If he defied custom, the ancestors would be angry, and then nothing would go right with his people. He would have to send Tandeka back to her father, a grievous thing to do to a woman once married. All would know, and despite her youth and beauty, no man would take her as his wife again. Yet he could not do otherwise.

Anta waited until his father was alone before he went to him. "Do not believe what is being said," he begged. If his father would give the order, he would take Tandeka into hiding, and no one would know were his father to visit her. Khwane praised him for his loyalty.

"She is near to my heart, and it is pain to lose her. Another man might dare to do as you say, but I cannot. I must obey custom." Anta saw his father's grief. He learned that day what strength and self-discipline it took to be a great chief.

At dawn, when Tandeka opened the door of her hut, she found a twig of the *mabope* plant lying outside. It was a notice to her that she was to leave the Great Place, or her hut would be burned to the ground.

Tandeka gathered up the few things that she would take on her journey. Grateful that no one was outside the huts to see her go, she departed, water-pot on her head, driving before her the cow of the home which she had brought with her as a bride from her father's place. Her sons belonged to her husband, and she left them to be reared by the other mothers. Her gait was almost leisurely as she turned toward the path to the stream. Her face showed neither anger nor resentment. She had been found guilty of the worst of evils, and she accepted her guilt, though she could not remember doing anything wrong. Perhaps it was in her sleep that she had caused harm to Nomaliso. One did not always know what one's spirit did in the night. She was fond of the girl, but it was true that at times she had felt hate for Balakazi and had tried to hide it. This hate had grown with each small disagreement, each time Balakazi boasted that she had more daughters than sons. She had nursed this grudge within her. How could she not believe that she was guilty when Gedja had found it to be so?

The door of the great hut was closed as she passed it. From the dark interiors of the other huts the wives watched in silence, filled with uneasiness because the enemy had been found within their very midst. Was she not someone close to them, someone who had worked their fields and sat with them to share their food? True, it was hard for Tandeka to be without daughters. But was not the life of any woman hard, and hardest of all to share the one she loves with another person? Every wife knows jealousy. Jealousy comes from the heart, they told themselves. Then who among them might not do as Tandeka had done? Whom else should they distrust and fear?

When he saw Tandeka leave her hut, Anta ran to the cattle fold and stood by the hedge where he could watch her. He dared not speak to her lest he be accused of having had a hand in the bewitchment. It filled him with pity and sorrow to see her sent away. Yet he wondered if perhaps she had been guilty, if something had caused her to do this evil thing. Now he understood why it was said that one did not have to fear strangers but only those living within the same home. They were the persons who knew all about you and had reason to do you harm. The fact that he himself was not safe from witchcraft struck terror in his heart. But he knew there was nothing he could do about it. From now on he must live with the thought.

chapter 7

Anta woke the next day with a sense of foreboding. His first thoughts were of the cattle. Among the older boys whoever rose earliest went out of habit to inspect the cattle fold. For Anta the best part of the day was this twilight hour before the dawn. His people called it the hour of the cattle horns, for then a man, bending low, can see the horns of his oxen black against the eastern sky. Today, driven by a feeling that all was not well, Anta seized his knobbed stick and rushed from the hut.

A heavy mist hung over the hillside. The gate of the fold was ajar, as if blown open by the wind. Diko must have neglected to fasten it securely, he thought. Once before, when this happened, two of the oxen had got out during the night but fortunately had strayed no farther than the stream.

Closing the gate, Anta stood for a moment, listening to the sighs and sounds that came from the fold. The voices of the ancestor spirits were speaking through the sleeping cattle, but what they were saying only a diviner could interpret. Through the drifting mist he could see the shapes of the animals as they rested on the ground. Going quickly from one group to another, he called to his ox, softly at first. "Big Forest!" he cried, his voice rising anxiously. The great, bulky shapes hardly stirred. In the fields, when it was misty and difficult to see the animals, he would call his ox by name and Big Forest would bellow, making it easy to find him. Suddenly he knew that Big Forest was missing. He ran to the stream, but the ox was not there. He could do nothing but return to the cattle fold and wait.

With the first rays of the sun, as the mist slowly thinned, Anta began to search for the tracks of his ox. So familiar to him were those hoofprints that he could usually pick them up without too much difficulty and follow them through a maze of tracks. Now they were the only fresh ones leaving the fold. There were footprints near the gate which led back to the huts, the direction from which they had come. Had someone opened the gate and deliberately driven out his ox? Anta dismissed the thought. No one could have managed this without causing a commotion among the cattle and attracting attention. What then could have made Big Forest so restless as to wander off on his own? Was he bewitched? Was it Tandeka's doing? He could not bear to think of that. Even so, he must find him. Big Forest might not be far away.

At the turning where the herd boys met each morning, he saw Maboni standing, as if waiting for him. His friend did not answer his greeting. He seemed remote yet intense, in a way that had become familiar to Anta.

"You must go to the place where the thorn grows thickest," said Maboni. "You must go alone." He had never been away on his own, thought Anta. It would take four days or more to reach the mimosa thorn country, and his father was not likely to give his permission unless Maboni could convince him. They must go to his father and tell him what had happened.

Khwane look troubled. "Is it the work of an enemy?" he asked Maboni.

"That is not what I see," Maboni replied.

Still, thought Khwane, I cannot let Anta go up into the mountains. It is unsafe. "I will send someone with him," he said.

"He must go alone," Maboni repeated gravely.

And Khwane said no more because it was known that Maboni always saw the truth. He can see far, Khwane said to himself; if he becomes an *igqira*, he will be a very great one.

Drawing his ochered blanket more closely around his body, Anta hurried off. Ahead the grassy tracks, wet with dew, glistened in the early light. All day long, past the cultivated fields in the valleys between the hills, he followed the trail of flattened grass left by the hooves of his ox. He saw the distant mountains, the seemingly endless way. Every step carried him farther from home.

At sundown he left the trail in order to seek shelter for the night at a group of huts near the top of a
ridge. From the hillside he could see the hedge of
closely planted aloes which ringed the cattle fold. He
had come to the place of his mother's people.

Soft gray spirals of smoke were rising from the
courtyard, and he watched them uncurl over the
huts and drift into the valley. The acrid smell of the
dung cooking fires filled the air with a pleasant tang.
He entered the courtyard as the last of the oxen
were being penned and the older boys, throwing
aside their blankets, were readying themselves for
the evening milking. The empty calabashes which
they would fill stood in a row near the gate of the
cattle fold.

Shouts of welcome greeted him as he walked
across the courtyard to the great hut. His kinsmen
received him with warmth and sympathy. Big Forest
could not have strayed far, they assured him; tomorrow he would find the beast. Anta devoured the
chunks of boiled meat which they set before him
and chased it down with gulps from a gourd of sour
milk. Then he curled up on a reed mat in the visitor's hut and went to sleep.

In the early dawn, when he opened the door of
the mud-walled hut, the air outside was crisp and
inviting. From the doorway he could see the outlines
of the neighboring hills, their soft green slopes still
hidden in the half-light. Beyond the hills and the far-

thest ridges were the Nunge mountains. He knew that the mountains were covered with great dark forests and that below them, too distant for him to see, lay the thorn country. A terrible doubt and loneliness overtook him. How would he ever make his way there alone? Suddenly he noticed that the ground in the courtyard was damp, and he realized that it had rained during the night. The tracks of the ox were gone.

Slowly and deliberately Anta rolled up the sleeping mat and returned it to its place on the clay shelf in the wall. He went outside to see if his mother's brother was up so that he could tell him he was returning home. Although it was not yet daylight, there were signs of life in the courtyard. Dim blanketed figures were beginning to move from hut to hut. The cattle were becoming restless in the fold.

As Anta reached the great hut, the door, tightly shut all night, was flung open wide to let in some light and air. His mother's brother came out and, seeing him, said in a gentle voice, "Your father's ox will come, my son." He tried not to show that he was glad about the rain because the grasses would grow and the cattle would look fresh and clean. "If you go home now, he may be there already."

Anta hesitated. Other herd boys were very skillful in tracking a lost animal, and he would be ridiculed. On the spur of the moment he told his mother's brother that he was not giving up. "But what will you do? Where will you go?" was the reply.

"To the thorn country," said Anta, realizing that tracks or not, he would do as Maboni had said. He would go, and he would go alone. A plan was forming in his mind. He would seek the help of the old Khoikhoi herder who kept his father's cattle in the ravines of the Nunge mountains. But how to find him?

With a full milk sack he set out boldly. All morning he followed the narrow pathways over the hills, bearing north toward the mountains where the thorn grew. By midday the heat was relentless. Weary and dispirited, he rested for a while on the banks of a stream. He found himself longing to hear the cheerful shouting and singing of the mothers of his home. He missed his brothers and sisters. Never before had he felt so alone. And where could Big Forest be? What if he were hurt or unwell, with no one to tend him, no one to see that he had water and food. Anta stooped by the side of the path and picked a long stem of grass, then walked on, chewing and tugging at it.

In the afternoon distant claps of thunder reached his ears. Thunderheads appeared as if from nowhere, and soon great, loose rain clouds darkened the sky. Knowing how suddenly these storms could break, he decided to seek shelter at once. He had passed very few huts that day, but a short distance ahead he saw a homeplace perched on the top of a hill. When he arrived there, the courtyard was deserted, the huts were silent. The gate of the cattle fold stood wide open. He noticed that the ground inside had been newly smeared with dung. As he walked past, a number of young boys came out, their hands wet from the smearing. Looking as if they had been caught in the act, they ran away, all except one small boy who stood and stared. It dawned on Anta that the cattle fold had been smeared to hide the fact that a beast, a stolen beast, had been killed there. Then came the awful thought: Perhaps it had been Big Forest! He asked the little boy to show him the skin of the slaughtered animal. And behind the hut where the calves were kept, spread out on the ground to dry, was a black-and-white stippled hide. Big Forest! But wait, the forelegs were not black. And now, as he looked more closely, he saw that the hide did not have the mark of his father's cattle. In the courtyard he was met by the head of the family, who appeared ill at ease. Although he was given the customary hospitality, he felt he was unwelcome.

He journeyed on, farther, ever farther from the places of the people. As the ground under his feet turned rocky, he knew he had reached the foothills of the mountain and was entering the dense mimosa thorn country.

A feeling of panic gripped him as he approached

the tangled thickets. He could not see ahead. His every move was filled with danger. At any moment he might come upon some savage animal—a lion, a leopard, even a wild cow. When he had made the journey with his father, the guide seemed to know every twist and bend. How should he go?

Starting out carefully, Anta glanced back often to see what the trees and rocky outcroppings looked like from the other side so as to recognize them should he have to turn back. After a long climb he came to a rock-strewn area bare of trees, where he rested briefly. Later, near a big rock, he saw footprints leading the same way he was going. The footprints were his own. He started out anew, fixing in his mind the more noticeable things he was passing: two flat-topped mimosa trees, a large gray ant-heap with a crooked mound, and a patch of tambookie grass. His uncertainty grew because soon he was trying to decide whether these were the same objects he had passed earlier. When for the second time he came across his own footprints, he knew he was lost.

The thought filled him with a terrible fear. Animals would eat him in the night, and even if he lived till morning, he might never find his way. The sun was setting. He must do what he could while the light lasted. He gathered dry twigs and, rubbing two sticks together until there were sparks, started a fire. Then he lay down in the sleeping place he had chosen: a slight dip in the ground with a large rock behind—and the little fire to keep the wild beasts away.

At daybreak, when he woke, his mood had changed. He bound his blanket and the milk sack flat against him. He must force a path through the bushes instead of going around them in circles. Despite the giant bone-white thorns of the mimosa, the thickets were not as impenetrable as they looked. He remembered his father saying that a mimosa without thorns would be like a polled ox.

Climbing steadily, he watched for small animals like rock rabbits that he might knock down. All at once two small birds flew up in front of him and an instant later, stunned by his throwing stick, dropped to the ground. He built a little fire of dry sticks at the spot where they lay, and to save them from charring away to nothing, he put them on the fire feathers and all, cleaning them only after they had been cooked. It took him only a moment to eat, and he was still crouching by the fire when he spotted a game trail which ran like a narrow tunnel through openings in the undergrowth. On hands and knees he followed the trail, hoping that it would take him to a drinking place at a stream. He was exhausted and had to stop more and more frequently. The trail led upward along the rocky side of the mountain, winding between the boulders, clumps of trees, and bush. At the place where the slope was steepest,

Anta looked down, and directly below him in the ravine he saw a riverbed.

Slowly, torturously, through bush and tangled vine, the scent of the wild jasmine heavy in the air, he descended to the floor of the ravine. There were many good drinking places along the river, and many tracks, tracks of cattle. He could tell that they were this morning's tracks because even in the soft, moist ground near the river's edge the water had not yet oozed into all the prints.

Excited, he followed the cattle tracks through the downtrodden grass. He was forced to go slowly. Near the river the stems of the tambookie were as thick as reeds. Also, he had to go quietly in order not to betray his presence. Away from the bank the thickets grew so dense that he could not tell when he might come upon the herd. Nor could he know whose cattle these might be. He dared not let himself hope that he had found the old Khoikhoi's herd, for these might not even belong to his father. Other men, wealthy in cattle, liked to hide part of their herds.

He moved cautiously up the side of the ravine. The mimosa thickets became fewer, and the light stronger. The rank grass ended abruptly, and he came to the edge of a clearing. There he saw them: a mixed herd of cattle resting on the ground, chewing, dreaming. All at once he caught their grassy, milky smell, a smell that reminded him of sweet pastures and his father's place. He restrained the impulse to go to them.

At first he saw no herdsmen, but then he made out the small, still figure of a man, almost merged with his surroundings. Staring hard, he recognized the slight build, the head grizzled with age, the garments of wildcat skins. It was the old Khoikhoi herder.

chapter 8

"Good day, Old Father," Anta shouted in the sharp, click tongue of the Khoikhoi people. Without waiting for a response, he stepped out of the thickets.

Immediately five oxen rose from their resting places on the outskirts of the herd and, forming a half circle, moved toward him. Anta drew back. The oxen came nearer, silent but menacing. They would surely attack him. There was a shrill whistle. Hearing the command of their keeper, the oxen stopped abruptly and returned to the herd. Anta walked into the clearing.

He was halfway across when he heard the roar of an animal, and through a cloud of dust he saw a huge dark shape bearing down on him. What had gone wrong? Why was the old man not stopping the beast? It was charging like a bull gone mad. As he turned to run, the animal halted, raised his head, and gave a long-drawn bellow. There was no mistaking the deep voice of Big Forest. Rushing forward, Anta flung his arms around his ox, shouting his name over and over, while Big Forest responded with sniffs and snorts. Feeling the warmth on his face from the ox's breath, Anta put his head still closer, drawing in long drafts of the sweet cattle odor. He was stroking Big Forest's back, passing his hands wonderingly over his smooth hide, when the old herder came up beside him.

"We have been waiting for you," he said.

"This is my ox," Anta cried excitedly. "I do not know how he got here, but I shall take him home."

"And how will you do that?" replied the old man.

Anta paused. He had not given thought to the fact that his ox was not broken to lead. "Tomorrow I will return and ask my father to send someone with me to bring him home."

"Even if someone helps you get your ox home, he will run away again," the old man said. "Stay until the ox is ready to go." It was difficult for Anta to accept this. How could he stay on without his father's permission? "Your father will know where you are," said the old herdsman.

Later, as they were sitting around the evening fire, the old man explained Big Forest's appearance among his herd. Although Anta had known his ox was not from the homeplace, he now learned that his father had sent for it out of the herd which he had put with the old man. The ox had been bred from cattle that had known no human other than the old herdsman. Big Forest had come home. "But," said the old man, "he would not have left you if you had tamed him."

He had always been good to his ox, Anta answered. He had taught him to respond to the sound of his voice, and Big Forest had shown no sign of wildness. If he approached while the cattle were grazing in the fields, Big Forest would leave the herd and come to him. At home he came to eat out of his hand. Anta could not understand what the old man meant.

"It is the wildness within that you have not tamed," said the old herdsman. "Tame him. Then he will become your ox."

"But how will I do it, Old Father?" Anta asked.

"You must begin with your own ox nature," the old man said.

And so the taming of Big Forest started. Anta had to teach himself to rise early and go to his ox even when he wanted to curl up more tightly. At daybreak he stirred the remains of the fire, warmed his hands, and walked to the place where the cattle were sleeping under the trees. Silently he sat near Big Forest each morning until, on the fourth day, the ox seemed to wake the moment he appeared. Of his own the animal rose from his resting place and followed him into the clearing. The mist swirled low around them, at times enveloping Big Forest. "I will not lose you, fine ox," Anta called reassuringly.

For days the old man watched them before proceeding to show Anta how an ox must be trained. He made a rope from thongs of hide and tied it around the animal's horns, so that Anta could lead the beast. "The skin of one ox tames another," said the old man. But Big Forest resisted it with all his might. For the first time Anta saw his docile ox turn rebellious. As the animal tried frantically to run away, Anta was forced to pull hard and even to use a whip. Long hours passed as he tried to make the ox understand what he wanted him to do. Speaking to the animal in a firm voice, he turned him slowly, first to the left, then to the right. After four days he could lead him in a circle. At last Anta removed the rope, and without it they walked around and around. Now and then Big Forest turned his head to look back at him, or Anta turned to look at Big Forest, until it was no longer clear whether he was following the ox or the ox was following him. They were one. Elated, he led Big Forest to a noisy little stream, and together they drank the cool, clear waters.

The nights became colder, and in the mornings frost lay thick on the ground. The pods on the acacia trees turned black. Each day, after working quietly with groups of cattle from the herd, the old man helped Anta train his ox. He tied him to the horns of the leader bull, and Big Forest followed the huge black-and-white beast, learning to obey the old herdsman's signals. Anta watched carefully until it was time to train him on his own, continuing in the old man's way.

Hissing short words at him, he ordered his ox to lie down. He whistled through his teeth, making piercing sounds as a signal to Big Forest to run toward him. He led him into the thickets and taught him to stay. With the koo, koo, kook-kooo of the dove, which he had learned from the old man, he called him from afar, while he waited on the slopes for his ox to find him. Then he would take him all the way to the bed of the ravine to feed on sweet grass among the trees.

Big Forest grew sleek. Anta imagined himself at home, watching the oxen come into the fold and hearing his friends say that none was as fat as his. "Ox, oh ox, I admire you," he chanted. And he brushed Big Forest with a rough stone until his body shone brilliantly.

Evenings were spent in the intimacy of the fire, listening to the old man tell about the wars of the Khoikhoi. It was his own people, he said, who had given refuge to Anta's father after his quarrel with Oba. Even then, as a young man, Khwane had shown the qualities of a chief, he said, and he had come to serve him, believing him to be destined for great things. The old man talked proudly of the herd which Khwane had left in his care. Their numbers had multiplied many times over, yet never had one been taken. His old eyes lit up whenever he mentioned cattle thieves. Those who had come upon the herd unexpectedly had been dealt with by the cattle themselves. And he described how the last such intruder had been trampled by three cows when he unwittingly approached a thorn bush where they had hidden their calves.

But how had he taught so large a herd to respond to his signals, Anta asked repeatedly. Here the old man would smile gently and say, "The cattle and I understand one another." Anta was ready to believe that the old one had special powers which enabled him to lead them.

Living so close to the herd, his nostrils filled more than ever with the odor of cattle, Anta was at peace with his world. During his months in the mountains he had come to accept the old man's way of life as his own. It was a rude surprise when the old hersman suggested that he accustom his ox to carry him on his back, so that he could ride home. Yet he had caught himself thinking about home of late. He had left just before the big harvest, when the corn was ripe for cutting. Now winter was past, and the cicada was singing in the long grass again. At home his people would be planting their crops. They would see him with his ox and know that the two of them belonged together, that they shared everything, that they could smell each other from afar.

When it came time to mount his ox, he found he could not do it in a leap. Big Forest stood high, and he had to lean his stomach against the animal's side, raise his leg over, and heave himself up. Then, too, it was hard to stay on. The ox's skin was loose and slippery, but once Big Forest started to sweat, it was easier for Anta to keep his legs tight against his body. Broken to the use of a rope around his horns, Big Forest quickly accepted the burden of a rider.

At his departure a day later the old herdsman presented Anta with his blanket of animal skins, sewn with sinew. It was the old man's most valuable possession, that and the long knife which he carried always. He had allowed Anta the use of the blanket all winter, while he had kept warm with garments of hide and fur. Without it Anta could not have withstood the severe cold of the mountains. During the day he had worn it as a mantle, hairy side turned inward, strapped across his chest with a thong. At night he had rolled up in it, covering himself from head to foot as they slept underneath an overhanging rock. Now he could use it to make a firm seat for riding. He threw the blanket over Big Forest's back and fastened it tightly.

"Go well, my son," the old man said.

"Stay well, Old Father," Anta replied.

chapter 9

For the first two days of the journey the going was rough. Slowed by the overhanging trees with their trailing gray lichen, the outcroppings of rock, and the dense thorn that covered the slopes, Anta had to make his way on foot, climbing and clambering, while Big Forest followed steadily behind him, stepping carefully with his firm, neat, bucklike tread. Then, as they were leaving the mountains, Anta began to ride his ox.

They emerged in a burst of sunshine onto the green, grassy plains to find the hillsides bright with red aloes and clusters of blue plumbago. Used to the darkness of the ravines and to seeing nothing but trees and thickets, Anta felt a surge of joy at the beauty and familiarity of his own hill country.

Never before had he seen such a profusion of aloes. They must have been flowering all winter while he was away. Stirred by memories of early boyhood, he alighted at the first stand of aloes he came to, and after breaking off a stalk with several blooms on it, he sucked the nectar from the tip of each flower—good for only two or three sucks before it turned bitter. These were sweet as honey because of the few drops of dew still on them. At the nearest stream he halted again and washed the red stains off his face and mouth.

Knowing that Big Forest did not like to be hurried, he stopped himself from pushing on too eagerly. Each morning he allowed his ox as much time as possible to graze and to chew. Big Forest was an affectionate beast. At night he would come and lie on his side by the fire next to Anta. Curled up against him, Anta could hear his ox breathing and could feel the rise and fall of his flanks.

On the third day he thought he saw gray-brown circles on the top of a distant ridge. He was not sure at first, for they looked so much a part of the ridge itself. And then he knew. It was a group of huts, their round walls made of mud, and like antheaps, they looked as if they had grown out of the earth on which they stood. He would pass many more before his journey was over.

From the cattle fold Diko heard the excited shouts and peered through the brushwood gate. The sight of Anta riding into the courtyard on the back of his ox was almost more than he could bear. The children were crowding around him, crying, "Where have you been?"

"I've been with my father's herds," Anta replied. Press as they would, he said no more. The slanting light of the sun gleamed warm and golden on the ox, on Anta, smiling and at ease.

The hour when all things are beautiful, thought Diko. Then and there he knew he hated his brother.

Anta dismounted in front of the great hut, and his mother ran out to greet him. Balakazi did not ask questions because she had accepted her husband's explanation. "He is herding for me in a far place," Khwane had told his people. She had ignored the talk of the women and the whisperings of Thubisi: "It is Tandeka's work. First the daughter of the great house, and now the ox and the son."

Khwane had permitted Anta's long absence only because Maboni had come to him, saying, "He is safe. I see him in the thorn country." He had thought at once of the old herdsman and guessed that the ox had returned. Were it not for that, he would have sent men up into the mountains to search for Anta and bring him home. But it had caused him to reflect further. A stay in the mountains with the old one could only be good. He had already allowed Anta more than was the custom, but he was the great son who must succeed him. Precisely because he himself was a commoner who had become a chief, Khwane felt impelled to bolster Anta lest one day he be challenged. Yet he did sometimes wonder whether he was doing the right thing.

Reluctant to leave the cattle fold, Diko brooded.

All his life he had had to accept that although he was the eldest son, Anta would become chief. As if that were not enough, his father favored Anta openly, giving him the gift of an ox after the rites whereas he himself had received a heifer. He had been deeply wronged. Why does my father do all these things for Anta when he does not deserve them? And why should Anta have been sent to do herding for him? Possessed with the thought that Anta knew more than he, Diko determined that one day he would find out where he had been.

He wanted his own ox, he informed his mother that same day; he wanted Manzányama, Black Water, a beast out of her herd. He knew that the house cattle given to her by his father were hers to do with as she pleased. She would not turn him down because she, too, resented Anta. She, the right-hand wife, knew what it was like to take second place to Balakazi, Anta's mother, the more so since she believed that she stood first among the older wives in Khwane's affections and that it was only the counselors who had picked out his great wife; otherwise, he would have chosen her. Because of this, thought Diko, he, her firstborn, the tallest and strongest of Khwane's sons, was not his father's principal heir. Yet it was she who had filled him with the idea that it was still possible for him to be his father's successor. It had happened before, she told him, that a chief had preferred his right-hand son. In his appeal to her, Diko was counting on his mother's rancor.

And so he became the owner of Manzányama, a black ox with horns *enxhele*, one horn pointing to the ground, the other straight up into the air. When Black Water was a calf, the horns of a slaughtered ox had been fitted over his own soft, pliant horns to make them grow into this shape. His horns were dangerous but much admired.

Black Water was an impatient animal, ever ready to stab or kick even those who worked with him daily. In the pastures he stood aloof, an unusual-looking ox with yellow eyes and twisted horns. As a three-year-old he had shown himself to be so ill-tempered a creature that Diko's mother had placed him with her brother, who for a year now had been his keeper. Though Diko was sure that he could handle the young ox himself, he was content that for the time being the animal should remain at the place of his mother's brother.

Anta was eager to tell his father about his months with the old Khoikhoi herdsman. In describing his journey to the mountains, he mentioned where he had stayed the second night and his suspicion that a stolen beast had been slaughtered there. To his surprise he learned that the head of the home was being accused of just such a thing. The charge had been brought months ago, said his father, but because the counselors of the neighborhood were not satisfied, the case was being referred to him. Tomorrow it would be settled in his court. "You must be there," Khwane told Anta.

To raid for cattle was one thing, Anta realized; to steal a beast was another. A theft of an ox from a man of your own people would be punished. Although he knew that a herd boy's words were heeded, he was apprehensive at the prospect of speaking in court. Charms were often used to tie up the tongue of a witness, and he feared that he might become confused in his mind and speech.

In the morning the countryside was red with the ochered blankets of men streaming from far and wide to attend the chief's court. There are few things men enjoy more, thought Anta. Some of them were renowned for speaking in court. But not they alone, any one present would have the right to question him.

A man approached the courtyard, shouting loudly. When he was closer, Anta saw that it was Sonto, whom he knew only slightly. "I come to complain, I come to complain," Sonto called out at the top of his voice. He entered the courtyard, and waited.

"Of what do you complain?" was the response from a counselor, leaving the great hut.

"I complain about someone," Sonto shouted.

"Say on," said his listener, pausing briefly. "Say on."

Whoever chanced to walk through the courtyard repeated the inquiry, not stopping but throwing questions to Sonto as he passed by. In this way notice was given; the complaint lodged. When the counselors were ready, the court assembled in the open alongside the hedge of the cattle fold.

Forming a large half circle, the people sat down on the grass while Sonto and his group of witnesses seated themselves in front, where they could be seen by everyone. As Anta joined them, he saw the accused and his supporters arrive and sit down near him. Flanked by his counselors, Khwane sat on a leopardskin, facing them all.

After a brief statement Khwane called upon the owner of the missing beast to begin. This Sonto did at great length, his speech eloquent with grief at the loss of his favorite ox which had occupied the place of a son in his home. The people listened attentively.

"Describe the beast," interrupted a counselor at last.

"Where and when did you lose it?"

"How many beasts do you have?"

The questions came not only from the counselors but from the listeners.

"Did you try to find your beast?"

"Yes," he replied, "I followed the tracks of my beast to this man's place."

The accused was now called.

"Have you stolen my beast?" Sonto asked him.

"Did you steal this man's beast?" repeated one of the men, jumping up.

"You were seen taking it," another stood up to say.

The accused denied everything.

"Why were the tracks there if you deny it?" asked a counselor.

"I deny the tracks were there leading to my place."

"But they were there."

"I was away and know nothing about these tracks," said the accused.

He knew the law required him to prove that the tracks of the missing ox had led past his place. "If the tracks were there, they must have gone past," he contended. "The rain may have destroyed them farther on. Sometimes it rains in one place and not the other." In the excitement of the moment he unknotted his blanket and threw it aside. As he spoke, his eyes shone and his body swayed. Growing more and more confident, he rambled on, going far back into the past, bringing out old grudges, and talking about things that had nothing to do with the case. The people allowed him to have his fair say.

His speech is misty, said Anta to himself. Glancing around, he saw a few men looking up anxiously at the sun as if they feared that the court would finish late. Others wore a look of dignified indifference.

Even his father seemed to be dozing when all the time he was following every word.

Anta listened intently while the accused was questioned abut the meat seen at his place. If it was a sacrificial kill, as he claimed, why was the feast not reported to the chief? Who was present? Was the ox that was slaughtered born and bred in his herd? Here the accused hesitated—because his neighbors know his cattle, thought Anta. If it was acquired, then from whom? The cross-questioning proceeded; more witnesses were called.

When it was Anta's turn to speak, he saw the accused spit in his direction and mutter something under his breath. He is chewing the *mabope* leaf; he means to tie me up, thought Anta uneasily. But once he began, his fear fell away. In a warm and impassioned voice he told of his search for his missing ox. The cattle were not yet home when he arrived at this man's place, he said, nor was it the usual time for a kill. That was why he had become suspicious of the freshly smeared cattle fold. He spoke of his distress when first he had seen the hide of the slaughtered beast, then went on to describe in detail the color of the animal's forelegs and the shape of its horns.

"Did you see the earmark?" a counselor asked, pressing him.

"Yes," said Anta, "it was a cut in the shape of a swallow's tail."

"That is the mark of my beast!" cried Sonto immediately. And with this weighty evidence the charge was proved.

Within hearing of all, the counselors discussed the matter briefly among themselves, after which Khwane made the pronouncement. Looking straight at the accused, he said, "We are satisfied that you stole the beast."

When Sonto rushed up to kiss his hands and praise him, Khwane sent him off with a few men to collect the fine: ten beasts for himself and one for the court. The affair was at an end.

While the people went on to the feast in the courtyard, the counselors turned to Khwane and complimented him on the gift of eloquence which Anta had displayed. Khwane received their remarks with modesty. The words came from men who cherished their reputations for wisdom and oratory in his court. It pleased him that others were noticing Anta. Since his return a change had come over him, more than just the way boys seem to change after being away at the cattle posts. Anta had grown. Not only was he more manly and confident, but he was also showing qualities of leadership.

In the glances directed at him Anta saw that his father's men were regarding him with interest and respect, and he knew that this would win him friends. As he stood in the courtyard, watching the last of the people leave, Maboni arrived. He had come to tell Anta that his family had at last agreed to let him become an *igqira*. Tomorrow he was leaving to go and live with Gedja, who would teach him. She had already built him a hut. Anta felt a pang of sadness. Maboni's life would be different now, and he would seldom see him. Yet he was glad for his friend. "You must be what you are," he said thoughtfully.

chapter 10

At the Great Place there was to be a celebration. Nomaliso, the chief's daughter, was undergoing the rites. Along the narrow pathways worn by foot, Khwane's messengers came and went, bringing the news to the homes on the slopes of the hills. The people must be told because what was of interest to one was of interest to all. They would come for the dances and the feast and for the ox race without which the celebrations were not complete.

Nomaliso was already secluded in a hut set aside for the event. Wrapped in blankets, she sat behind a screen made of mats, hidden from the eyes of all but her attendants. These were the women who were instructing her and seeing to her needs as she carried out the rites that a girl must observe when she reaches the age of puberty. Nomaliso was glad to be fulfilling custom, glad to become a woman and be accepted by others. It was a happy occasion for her and for those around her.

The ceremonies would last a month, and Khwane intended to provide plenty of food. For the feast held in Nomaliso's honor on the day of her coming out he would slaughter his fattest cattle, and his show of generosity would be praised by the people. He knew that a rich man could not give grudgingly without losing his standing. Once the rites were over, Nomaliso would be eligible for marriage, and the bridewealth she would earn would more than restore the size of his herds. Girls bring wealth to their fathers.

Just as any man cares for his household, Khwane cherished his people, and in return he received their obedience and loyalty. They called him the herdsman of his country. And indeed, he thought of himself as a herdsman, boasting often of his skills. The beauty of a man is in the cattle, he liked to say. Khwane's heart was with his cattle. Except for those at the distant grazing posts, he knew them by name and by their bawling voices. He knew every spot on their hides, every turn of their horns. Every head was as familiar to him as the faces of his children. He knew the walk of a smooth fat cow, the jostling habits of his bulls. His watchful eye could tell at once whether an animal was resting or was unwell. "Bellow, oh black bull of the people of Vukuthu," he chanted as his favorite bull came out of the fold, and the bull would bellow at the top of his voice, then put his head down and low softly.

"Truly, they are brothers," his friends said admiringly.

However, he felt closest to his racing ox, uBhayilam, My Blanket, a red beast with horns that turned inward. Khwane lavished care and affection on his famous ox. No one was permitted so much as to lay a hand on him. But he had made it known that the day he died uBhayilam was to be killed, so that he could be wrapped in the skin of his favorite ox and be buried inside the cattle fold beneath the feet of his herd.

Having worked with many cattle, abandoning the ones that did not respond, Khwane had known at once that uBhayilam had the makings of a fine racing animal. Built for speed, his huge body high from the ground, he could be made to run at an astonishing pace. He had never been outrun; not only that, he left his rivals far behind. A noble beast, highstrung and sensitive, he had been taught to obey even the gestures of the herd boys. uBhayilam had both heart and training. With a keen sense of pleasure, Khwane thought of the honor his ox would bring him in the forthcoming race.

Anta visited Nomaliso in her hut, as a brother was allowed to do. Speaking through the screen of mats, he told her that he was preparing Big Forest for the race. It was not easy for him to think that his little sister would soon be ready for marriage. Someday she would be going away.

One afternoon the men met outside the cattle fold as usual, and squatting on the ground, they smoked their pipes and talked idly about the happenings of the day. At Sibi's place the black cow had stopped giving milk. At Kotongo's home a child had been bitten by a small brown spirit snake, and although it was harmless, Kotongo had killed a fowl to keep on good terms with the ancestors. uBhayilam, they said, seemed to sense there was going to be a race and was more high-strung than ever. An old man recalled a course so long and so rough that two famous oxen had dropped dead of exhaustion within sight of the finish. Then, just as his listeners were turning away from him, the speaker suddenly remarked that Anta, the chief's son, had been acting strangely. At dawn on three successive days he had seen him driving a small group of oxen across the ridge. The men were silent. They could not imagine what he might be doing.

Early one morning, even before the hour when the cattle begin to rise and their horns become just visible over the hedge, Anta had entered the fold, and moving quietly among the herd, he had roused Big Forest and three of his father's oxen. *"Vuka*, wake up," he called gently to them, and the oxen, hearing his voice, rose from the ground. Silently he led them out and, with Big Forest in front, drove them over the ridge and down onto the plains to a line of yellowwood trees. The next few mornings he had taken them there again, driving them as hard as he could to show them where the race would end. On the day itself Big Forest would have to run through the courtyard, keeping to the space between the huts and the cattle fold. In this a racing ox was not permitted to make a mistake. Anta felt sure that Big Forest would know where to run. Each time he had rewarded the oxen with some fine corncobs and had placed salt on the ground as a treat for Big Forest.

Nomaliso's seclusion was at last coming to an end. Every morning and evening throughout the month the married women had performed their dance. For the last six days the men had been dancing in the courtyard, and the thud of their feet could be heard over the singing and the beating of the cowhide. Today at sundown a beast would be killed for the final ceremonies; tomorrow the screen behind which Nomaliso sat and the rushes and grass used on the floor of her hut, would be set alight. And with the observance of this custom Nomaliso would leave her childhood behind her.

At sundown the men gathered at the cattle fold to await the return of the herds and to watch Khwane choose the beast of the burning of the mat. Standing at the gate, Khwane cast his eyes over the oxen as they trampled and pushed their way into the fold. Then an awful thing happened. For no apparent reason uBhayilam, his racing ox, suddenly stumbled, then went on through the gate with the other oxen. "uBhayilam chooses himself," said Khwane's brother in a low, shocked voice. The men glanced quickly at Khwane. An animal that chooses itself expresses the wish of the ancestors and must be taken. To defy the spirits would bring misfortune. A calamity was sure to follow; something would happen, they knew, if not to uBhayilam, then to the other cattle. Had Khwane forgotten that he had not yet made up for the strange death of the red-and-white ox, the beast that did not bellow? Usually the ancestors were willing to wait for an ox that had been promised to them, but perhaps they had become impatient. Surely Khwane knew what he had to do.

Khwane well knew. He knew that the ancestors were seldom slow in showing displeasure, particularly when a man failed to honor custom. But, he wondered desperately, how can one give up a beast that is a part of oneself? He hesitated; then, ignoring the incredulous looks of the men, he calmly selected a different animal of the same color, a fat young ox with strong horns. Without further incident he completed the kill. Anta watched with amazement. Had his father not told him that a man must obey custom? But what if it had been Big Forest?

He was awakened during the night by an unusual commotion among the animals, which were lowing and bellowing in the cattle pen. As he ran to see what it was, his father and a few men rushed from their huts with their spears and sticks. They found the cattle milling and stamping on the ground at the place where the young ox had been killed. Later, roused for a second time, they discovered that two of the oxen had been fighting and, having broken the gate, had gone out. Nothing like this had ever happened before. By morning everyone knew that Khwane's cattle were dissatisfied.

Hlubi, the *ixhwele*, arrived early to prepare for the race, bringing with him medicines that would protect the cattle of the home from witchcraft. He had already examined the course and had dug powdered roots into the ground along the way. Such an event at the Great Place would bring all the people, and Hlubi was anxious to please his chief. He supplied Khwane with a powerful ointment which he was to rub on the horns and tail of his racing ox, and for the runners who would accompany the ox, he brought pieces of tree bark they were to carry with them.

Several times during the week Anta had caught sight of Hlubi, who appeared to be waiting around. At last Hlubi approached him. "If you come to me," he said, "I can give you medicines to make the other oxen run slower. I can make your ox win." He does not care who wins, thought Anta. Although he could have used Hlubi, he had felt the need to consult someone else. First, however, he had to pay for it. With the gift of two hens from his mother's people he had been able to go to Ngubengcuka, who lived near them. From him he had received potent plants, good for many purposes but effective against witchcraft when used in a certain way. Therefore, when Hlubi approached him, he did not tell him that he had already burned herbs and roots, which he had shown to no one, that he had mixed the ashes with grass and had fed it to his ox to make him run faster. He himself had taken a potion, an emetic, which made him violently sick but which, in so doing, had made him lighter so that he could run more swiftly beside his ox. And he would look beautiful to the people. Big Forest would look beautiful, too, because he had wiped his horns and painted them in bands of white clay and ocher.

He knew that Hlubi had given Diko some crushed leaves, telling him to burn them and make sure that Black Water inhaled the smoke. Not everyone had consulted an *ixhwele*. Pinda, who could not afford one, had rubbed pig's fat on his legs and stick and on the legs of his racing ox. It would be a question of whose medicines were the strongest. Anta was hopeful. Yesterday in the pasture he had seen an *umcelu*, bird of good omen, perched on the back of his ox.

The day's ceremonies were due to begin when a man named Vukili arrived with his racing ox. Close behind him came his runners, driving a herd of cattle, perhaps a hundred head. Although Vukili was not from these parts, he was well known to the people. In his own neighborhood, where his ox had never lost a race, both ox and owner were highly acclaimed. uGquma babaleke, Frightening Bellower, was a red ox with a white face, a white belly, and a spot of white on one foot that was greatly admired. He had fine horns that swept backward. His sudden entry caused a stir among the people.

At Nomaliso's hut the burning of the grass screen and mat was the signal for the final burst of revelry. The men and women thronged the courtyard, their mantles orange in the sun. Their black turbans were folded in high, loose shapes, and they wore layer upon layer of bead necklaces and armbands. In noisy celebration they danced and sang. There was meat for all. Khwane had provided amply for sacks of curd, and his wives had prepared pots of boiled millet and strong drink brewed from the new corn.

Now, while the feasting was in progress, the racing oxen were brought to be shown to the guests. Khwane's ox was praised to the sky, and no one cared to remember that he had been called by the spirits. Only Frightening Bellower was a worthy rival, the people said. Black Water had raced and done well but was an animal they did not trust; Big Forest could be counted on to do his best, but he was inexperienced. Antheap-Gorer was unpredictable; his aggressive ways had made it necessary for Pinda to poll his horns. Sibi's light red ox, Thrower-Down, was stubborn and unreliable; Herd-Keeper, they said, never performed well, yet Sonwaba entered him in every race.

While the oxen were paraded, the guests,

mellowed by the brew became more and more eloquent as they described the color of each beast and the shape of its horns. Watching over the proceedings, Khwane at last gave the order for the animals to be driven off. "*Éwe*, to be sure, cattle fill the heart," he intoned.

"*Éwe*, indeed," murmured his guests.

chapter 11

The racing oxen were taken to the starting point at the edge of the Gonogono wattle trees. Each contender would be accompanied by cattle from his home herd because even a trained ox runs best with others. These animals had been rounded up earlier and were grazing near a stream in the vicinity of the grove. The bulls were excluded. With their instinct for being the master they would disrupt the race.

Groups of relatives and friends began to station themselves along the course. Among them were the runners, who, in relay, would keep pace with the cattle and guide them. Anta had thought carefully about who would run with Big Forest. He had decided that Sidalo should start. Two of Sidalo's friends, who were good runners, would take the other relays, and he himself must run last. As he went to his position, trailed by his brothers and sisters, he saw his father leave the Great Place with his counselors and set off in the direction of the finish.

When Vukili's cattle arrived at the grove of wattle trees, Frightening Bellower knew there was to be a race and started to run. Because lining up was impossible, this was taken as the signal that the race had begun. Without waiting for their own cattle to reach the starting point agreed upon, the runners of the other groups shouted and whistled to get them going.

But something unusual was happening. One group of cattle had been left behind. The young men were making frantic efforts but could not get the leader of the herd to run. Khwane's famous ox was refusing to race. "It is the ox that chose himself," said an elderly bystander. "Khwane should have given him up. He knows that nothing a man does escapes the notice of the ancestors. Sometimes they can be tricked over little things, but there is a limit to their good nature. Did Khwane really think he could get away with it?" The pushing, shouting, and coaxing went on, but when the runners found that it was useless, they drove the ox and his home herd back to the Great Place.

Frightening Bellower had an easy lead until he was forced to slow down at the Mvenyane rivulet, where Diko's ox, Black Water, caught up with him. As the two groups of cattle crossed the shallow stream, the next relay of men took over.

They raced in the open, on the wide grassy plains, the runners guiding the animals along a course which avoided the broken ground where the gullies cut deep into the red earth. The cattle were staying in groups, the racing oxen in front.

Neck outstretched, his backward-sweeping horns laid low, Frightening Bellower was moving along at a swift pace when, on reaching a clump of mimosa, he seemed to stumble as if he had stepped into a small hole. Were this so, he would almost certainly have broken a leg. The onlookers shouted that Diko must have buried medicines there to try to make him fall. Vukili's supporters became furious. They shouted encouragement to Frightening Bellower. "Come up, Whitespot, take the lead, we've known you long!"

But their cries were lost in the noisy whistling that came from Diko's men. "Bellower, you are covered with the dust of the leader. Where is your white spot now?" they yelled scornfully. All the way to the Umatuta River the runners of the two groups kept on hurling insults at each other.

On the bushy banks of the river the race once more came to a halt while the herds crossed the rocky shallows where the water was no more than a thin stream. Here Big Forest caught up with the main contenders as Sidalo's friend stood waiting, ready to run with him.

It was not long after this that Sonwaba's runner tripped and fell. Moments later his ox seemed to tire and slow to a trot. Scarcely ten paces from the spot, at a tall stand of spiky aloes, Sibi's light red ox suddenly turned around and galloped back in the direction from which he had come.

A wave of excitement was mounting as the spectators ahead turned their full attention to the two in the lead, Black Water and the ox with the red-and-white face. Foaming at the mouth, Frightening Bellower was straining hard. Vukili took over the next relay, and as he started to run, he chanted praises. "Beast whose bellowing makes the children come out of their huts," he sang. On hearing his owner's voice, the stouthearted ox redoubled his efforts. Coming up on the left, he ranged himself beside his opponent, and the two galloped at full speed, leaving their runners behind. Hard pressed, his yellow eyes and nostrils wide with fierceness, Black Water sensed that his competitor might outdo him. He veered to the left, narrowing the gap between them. Then, all at once, with a quick movement of his head, a sweep of his upright horn, he slashed at his rival. As the wounded ox stood swaying, Black Water attacked again, and using his murderous horn in a swift succession of strokes, he gored Frightening Bellower to death.

There was a hush, then shouts and wild applause. Above the tumult of voices Diko's friends could be heard to yell, "Great race, which sprays the course with blood!" Unrestrained in their admiration, they lauded Black Water for the intelligence he had shown in eliminating his rival. Vukili's people were enraged by the calamity which had befallen their ox. Tempers flaring, the young men raised their sticks, both sides shouting abuse at one another.

Vukili stood beside his ox and wept. Praising him in death, he chanted, "Here lies the excellent one of the home, pierced by the spear of envy—*Laf' indune' elihle lakowethu, libinzwa likrele lomona.*"

Unnoticed, Big Forest streaked ahead toward the Great Place. Long before he came into view, those who had waited there after the feast saw a cloud of dust gradually drawing closer. When they could hear the shouting and whistling of the runners, the women drew together and stood in groups to await the cattle. As soon as Big Forest and his herd entered the courtyard, the women broke into high-pitched ululations, trilling with their tongues, a cry ending in a great shout. They kept up the clamor, calling praises in the name of the clan. It did not distract Big Forest. He knew the right way to run. Moments later Black Water and his herd thundered into the courtyard after him. Bringing up the rear, Pinda's ox, Antheap-Gorer, became confused. Instead of staying in the open space between the huts and the cattle fold, he swerved to the right and ran between the huts. Antheap-Gorer was out of the race.

How was it, asked Pinda, that only Antheap-Gorer had lost his way? A good, experienced racing ox did not make this mistake unless someone had worked against him.

"Did you not notice," said one of his men, "that before the race, when the oxen were being shown, Sibi walked away. It was then that he did something. Now do you see what happened today?"

Crowding around him, Pinda's friends advised

him to consult a witchfinder as soon as the race was over. "Do you remember the wedding feast of the family of Mtoba, when Lolombela's ox ran the wrong way?" they reminded him. "It was proved after the race that there had been a bewitchment."

Down the broad slopes of the hill behind the Great Place the remaining oxen and their herds headed for the last stretch in which the race would be decided. On the plains below, Anta and Diko waited for the final relay.

As the racing oxen drew near, Anta saw that there were only two. Where is uBhayilam? he wondered. Where are the others? What can have happened? Then it is between Big Forest and Black Water! Anta rushed forward and ran beside Big Forest, shouting his praise. "Beautiful ox of my father, running like an antelope, doing miracles among people, they all look at you and admire you." Big Forest responded by running even faster.

Quick to the challenge, Black Water came up from behind and drew level with Big Forest. He turned toward him for an instant, lowering his horn, then passed him. When they saw him pull ahead, the onlookers burst into applause and recited his previous victories to urge him on. "At the coming of age in the family of Yakwaxhego you did wonders," they chanted.

Lining both sides of the course, the spectators roared in support of the two contenders, their excitement whipped to a frenzy by the news that Khwane had arrived and was watching from the hillside overlooking the winning post.

Just then Big Forest saw the row of yellowwood trees ahead and recognized it as the place where the race would end. With extraordinary exertion he tore off, leaped a ditch three paces wide, and kept going. Staying clear of his dangerous opponent, he passed him on the left, his home cattle streaking behind him. When they were far enough ahead, Big Forest swung to the right, and, as if in perfect understanding with his herd, he led them in front of Black Water and blocked off the path of his rival.

He reached the yellowwood trees gasping, hollow-flanked, and utterly exhausted. The herd boys were the first to crowd around him. "They thought you could not do it, big ox," they chanted. The people sang his praises, lauding him for his intelligence and insight. They called him a manlike ox, an ox of imagination, with the knowingness to act on his own. Khwane acclaimed his excellence.

In an ox race a man's honor and dignity are involved and the honor of his ox. It is not just the winning that counts. Anta looked at Big Forest, at his eyes, deep and dark, like gray stones in a mountain stream. Standing close beside him, he chanted, "My father's ox that runs like an antelope, no matter what, it will always be the same, tomorrow and tomorrow. I beside him. You see us. We are sons of one man."

He did not forget to praise the *ixhwele* whose medicines had been more powerful than those of his competitors. "I was not lost when I consulted Ngubengcuka, the chief of all medicine men, who defeated the Bull of the North," he exclaimed.

Knowing that the remark referred to him, Hlubi sought to excuse himself. "Roots are not always dug in the same place," he muttered irritably. Surely people could understand why one medicine was less strong than another. He was not at all pleased by the blow to his reputation or by the scowl on Diko's face.

Although Khwane bore his misfortune well, he brooded on the fact that his famous ox had refused to race. The ancestors were turning their backs upon him, he thought. Their displeasure had changed to wrath. Outwardly he remained calm, but when the guests departed, he sent for Gedja, the wise one, and asked her to find out from the spirits what it was they demanded of him.

After chanting and wild dancing, Gedja entered the great hut, followed by her attendants. Behind walked Maboni, in the white skirt of a learner. Gedja and her attendants squatted in a half circle, and with loud incantations she called up the spirits. She communed with them in silence; then, interpreting their wishes, she told Khwane what he feared most to hear. "You must shed blood," she stated. "The ancestors want your best ox."

Waiting outside in the courtyard, Anta saw Gedja

111

and the others leave the great hut. "It is not over yet," Maboni said to him.

At sundown the members of the Great Place gathered at the cattle fold to watch Khwane perform the rites. When his racing ox had been caught and trussed, Khwane passed his spear back and forth above the animal's body, between the front legs, between the hind legs, then once more around the same way. At the jab of the spear in his belly uBhayilam bellowed, calling the ancestral spirits. A murmur of approval rose from the onlookers because now it was in order for Khwane to proceed. And with a stab in the back of the neck Khwane completed the kill. By giving them what they had demanded, he appeased the ancestors.

For the first time in his life Anta saw his father weep. It was plain that he suffered even more over the death of his favorite ox than he had at the loss of Tandeka.

The race at Nomaliso's coming out was the topic of conversation for months. Anta and his ox became famous. People said they were one, they shared the same blanket. Anta was elated. His friends cautioned that a man must not be vain of the honor he has won. Diko said only, "My brother and his ox are praised today. But there is no ragwort that blooms and does not wither."

chapter 12

In the intimacy of the hut which the young men shared, even Anta noticed that Diko was sulking. At the place of his mother's brother, where he still kept Black Water, the herd boys said that he hardly spoke to them. Diko seemed to care only for his ox.

One morning, when Anta went early to the cattle fold, Diko rose and waited outside for him to return. Anta was glad to see that he was smiling.

"Let us race our oxen again, brother of the great house, just you and I," Diko said without further ado. "This time my ox will outrun yours." The proposal took Anta completely by surprise. As children they had raced the calves this way, never the oxen. Surely their father would not permit it. Besides, the thought of Diko's ox filled him with fear. Before he could think of something to say, Diko began to taunt him, belittling Big Forest. Again he dared Anta to pit his beast against his own.

Now that it was a question of honor, Anta accepted the challenge. He was suddenly confident that he could guide his ox and keep him a safe distance from the other. They arranged to meet the next day at the grove of wattle trees, where, boasted

Diko, they would soon find out whose was the better ox. "The matter is between ourselves. Tell no one," said Diko walking away.

In the morning Anta left for the pastures as usual. When his ox had grazed sufficiently, he turned him out of the herd, telling his friends that he was taking him for a run. He led Big Forest slowly until he was out of sight behind the hill. Then he set off in the direction of the Gonogono.

Arriving there, he saw Diko step out from the dark shadows of the wattle grove. When he called out a greeting, his half brother made no response. He must have been waiting long, thought Anta. Black Water was grazing nearby. He lifted his head to stare at them, one horn pointing straight into the air, and Anta saw a savage look in his wild yellow eyes. All at once he felt terror. It was as if he were seeing Diko and his ox together for the first time.

"We will race in the Split as far as the Mvenyane," said Diko impatiently. "I will give the sign." The Split was the name which the herd boys had given to the grassy stretch of ground between the twin hills. A level, narrow tract, it lay like a divide in a ridge that had been cut in half. Instead of the open plains, Diko had chosen this place to make sure that the two oxen would be running close together. He was hoping that his ox, if hard pressed, would attack.

Without speaking, they walked their oxen along

the edge of the Gonogono. Anta's fear mounted. When they came to the twin hills, Diko hurried forward to take up his position on the outer right.

Anta stood waiting beside his ox. He should never have agreed to this, he told himself, not here, in the Split. Big Forest was in mortal danger. Just as he was going to call out that he would not race, Diko shouted, and the oxen started to run.

In that moment Anta knew what he had to do. Sprinting to catch up, he ran along the middle of the course between the oxen, forcing Big Forest to keep on the left. He should do nothing to encourage his ox; rather, he hoped Black Water would get well ahead and stay in the lead.

To his dismay his ox took the field at top speed. Both animals were doing their best. They did not seem to mind running without their home herds, the way racing oxen usually do.

As Anta looked ahead along the unfamiliar course, wondering how much farther it was, he watched the oxen to see that neither was straying from his path. He could hear Diko's voice, harsh and angry, urging Black Water on. All at once he heard the sharp snap of a whip. Big Forest twitched his ears. What was Diko doing? As he turned his head to look, the ground gave under his feet, and he found himself lying in a ditch, groaning, one leg doubled beneath him.

The next he knew, Big Forest was standing over

him, snorting and bellowing, and Sidalo and his friends were there beside him. Lifting Anta, Sidalo noticed some small twigs on the grass. He bent down and examined the ground carefully. The ditch appeared to be similar to those caused by little gullies of water which cut into the plains. But this one had been dug. It had been covered over with branches and a layer of freshly cut grass. To judge by its size, it would have taken time to prepare, and the grass must have been added that very morning. Had Big Forest not been running so far on the left, he would have fallen too. Now Anta understood everything. He told them about the race. "It was Diko, but the ditch was for my ox," he said. Truly, Maboni had seen it long ago when he said that Big Forest would lead him into danger. And was it over now?

While they carried Anta home, Sidalo explained how they had found him. "We thought it strange when you went off. Then, when we were walking in the fields, we heard the bellowing of your ox, and when we came, he was with you."

At the stream within sight of the Great Place a group of small children were playing in the mud. Dropping their clay oxen, they ran to meet them, while a few raced ahead with the news. By the time the boys reached the top of the hill, Khwane was waiting. After taking them to the great hut, he sent word to Balakazi and to Hlubi. In the vegetable gardens all work ceased, and soon the great hut was so crowded that Hlubi had to push his way in. Known for his skill in mending broken limbs, he had come prepared, bringing with him strips of wood. When it was found that no bone was broken, the women turned their attention to the question that still had to be answered: Had witchcraft been used against Anta?

They asked their husband if they might seek out a witchfinder. Khwane told them that he would give his answer later. He had already sent two counselors to examine the place where Anta had fallen. On their return Thubisi heard of her son's infamy and knew that she would pay for it, not only through a forfeit of cattle but through the disgrace which he had brought upon the right-hand house. The next day she obtained Khwane's permission to visit her old father.

Diko did not come back to the Great Place. It was learned that he had stopped at the home of his mother's people and had told them that he was on his way to Oba.

chapter 13

Even as he saw Anta fall, Diko realized his mistake. He had thought only of harming the ox, of taking away from Anta's importance. He had forgotten that if his plot succeeded, the evidence would be there for all to see. It was a great offense to injure a beast and a greater one to injure a chief's son. He would be punished. His father would disown him and drive him out.

He knew that he could not hide among his mother's people, even if they dared let him stay. He could go to no one friendly to his father. Then to an enemy. To Oba. He had heard that he welcomed stragglers. Oba was not likely to give him up, nor did he think his father would demand his return. Indeed, he counted on his father to honor the custom which allowed a man to take refuge with another people.

He knew that Oba's Great Place could be seen from the summit of the Nunge mountains. And it was some four days later, while seeking his way through the Nunge, that he found a large group of cattle at a river.

From the maze of tracks on the bank he could tell

that this was the regular drinking place of the herd. There must be a cattle post nearby, thought Diko. He wondered whether these belonged to his father, but there was no knowing because the ravines were the best places of concealment for men who wished to hide their wealth. The cattle could even be Oba's.

When he thought about cattle posts, the old bitternesses welled up. His father had taken Anta to visit the distant posts, and not him. Now these same posts were a threat. If the herd at the river was his father's, the herdsmen might recognize him. He must be careful.

After tethering his ox to a tree near the bank, he found cattle tracks which led him up the steep side of the ravine. A sudden movement in the thickets startled him. Through openings in the bushes he saw an ox feeding on a patch of grass and more cattle grazing on the slope nearby. He proceeded cautiously so as not to frighten them. By the sparseness of scrub higher up he could tell he was coming to a clearing, but there was nothing to warn him that he was so close, none of the usual clamor of a cattle post. He came upon them abruptly—a great, silent herd resting under the trees.

From the edge of the clearing Diko stared in disbelief. In a large, flat area trampled smooth were hundreds of head of cattle, and no one to guard them, no one, that is, except an old, old man, whom he had not at first noticed. Garbed in animal skins the color of the ground and scrub, the old one was sitting motionless near a burned-out fire. Asleep or awake, thought Diko, this man cannot protect a herd. There was nothing to prevent him from driving off a few head of cattle on the spot. Then again, if he bided his time, here was an immense prize waiting to be captured. But who was the owner of this herd? Even as he watched them, the cattle began to turn their heads in his direction, sniffing the air. When he looked again, the old man was gone.

Retreating quickly, he went to the place where he had left his ox, his progress slowed by the other cattle, which were returning from the river. The animals were spreading out over the side of the ravine, and he had to go carefully to avoid them. He was anxious to move on so that he could reach the summit before sundown. It was dusk when at last he led his ox through the narrow pass of the mountain and found himself looking down on the plateau of Oba's Great Place.

His arrival was reported to Oba, and he was summoned to explain his presence. Oba granted the right of refuge, although he was not pleased at taking in the son of his old enemy. Shrewd enough to sense this, Diko knew that he must impress him immediately. "I know where there are cattle, thick as the mist on the mountaintop," he told Oba.

"Where did you see them?" Oba asked.

"On the other side of the Nunge," Diko replied. And Oba knew at once that they were not his own cattle. Without divulging their whereabouts, Diko described the herd he had discovered. He did not know the exact numbers because the cattle were not all in one place but were scattered in the bush. If Oba would give him a reward, he would bring him the cattle. Oba was no stranger to cattle lifting, or to the punitive raids that almost always followed. The owners of these will never rest until they have come for them, he told himself. But the one thing he could not resist was the lure of cattle. "Bring me the cattle first," was his reply. He gave Diko ten men to help round them up.

In the morning the men awoke to find the Great Place closed in by an unusually heavy mist. Rising from the ravines, it was drifting in thick masses over the huts and the cattle folds. Not only the peaks of the mountain but the whole Nunge range were hidden from view. This was no ordinary mist, they said; this was a mist that had been sent. And anyone who could work such powerful witchcraft was a most formidable enemy. Despite Diko's insistence on the need for haste, the men refused to leave their huts.

For two days the mountains and the plateau on which they lived remained covered by mist. On the third day, when it began to clear, the men reluctantly agreed to go. They set off in single file behind Diko and his ox.

Khwane called together his counselors and his people, presented the evidence, and, in the presence of all, disowned Diko as his son. The counselors urged Khwane to pursue him, saying that Diko's rivalry with his half brother would destroy the people. He had shown himself to be violent and unprincipled, yet just such a man, bold and fearless, would be likely to attract to him other restless young men. But Khwane wanted time to think. "This is not a thing to do quickly," he said. "A man has a right to take refuge. But it shall be dealt with."

Khwane was torn by the decision he must make. If he demanded Diko's return, there could be no punishment for him other than death. In the meantime, Anta must take his proper place and be seen as the great son. Though recovered from his injury, Anta was shaken and subdued. He would send him to the cattle posts to do the inspection for him.

A few days later Anta and his ox began the journey to the Nunge mountains once more. Carrying a stick with a leopard tail tied on the end to show that he was sent by Khwane, he stopped at the various cattle posts, where he received reports from the keepers on the numbers and condition of the herds. He could forget Diko's treachery for a time. And he was glad that his father had told him to go also to the old Khoikhoi herdsman and the secret herd.

Taking a shortcut, he avoided the impenetrable thorn and great rocks and reached the side of the mountain where the climb was easier. Never again would he become lost in the Nunge, thought Anta. Big Forest seemed to know where they were going. At the bottom of the ravine, near the sanctuary, he headed for his old drinking place at the river. But suddenly he stood still, his ears spread wide, nostrils quivering. Something was amiss. Anta crept forward, searching the scrub that grew close to the riverbank. He stopped short. Tethered to a bush was a black ox with horns *enxhele*. It was Diko's ox, Black Water. He hurried back and hid Big Forest in the thickets, ordering him to stay.

He went straight to the giant willow tree at the main drinking place of the herd, and there, where the huge tree roots trailed over the shallow bank, he saw Diko and a group of men. They were standing close together, staring attentively at the ground—at cattle tracks, no doubt. Then he saw Diko point up at the side of the ravine. It was enough for Anta.

When he reached the clearing with Big Forest, the sun was going down behind the mountain, and the deep shadows of the thorny acacias had spread over the open ground. In a brief while the ravines and precipices would be plunged into total darkness. Would Diko dare lead his raid at night?

"What shall we do?" he asked the old herdsman, after telling him about Diko and the men.

The old herder replied slowly. "The cattle can take care of themselves, of course; that is nothing. He will never be able to round them up. But he must not be allowed to return to Oba, nor any of the men with him, because they have seen the cattle. If it is left to the herd," he mused, "just possibly one of the men could escape. We need a plan to make sure that this does not happen. We have until morning," the old man added. "Diko will not try anything tonight. He will wait for the hour of the cattle horns."

On the riverbank Diko sat huddled with his men, telling them how he proposed to capture so great a booty. When first he came upon the cattle, he said, he had thought of spying on the post to learn the name of their leader, so that he would be able to call it from the distance, knowing that the rest would follow. But after seeing the size of the herd, he had to think up another plan. And that was why he had brought along his racing ox, Black Water. At daybreak, when the cattle were still all in one place, he would quietly drive his ox into the herd to mingle with them. Then he would give his ox the command to run, and the whole herd would stampede with him out of the clearing. The cattle would think it a race. After that they could be rounded up and driven over the mountain ridge.

Listening to Diko in the eerie stillness at the bottom of the ravine, the men were not convinced. They were terrified at the thought of spending the night in this place, and uneasy from the start, they now felt sure that the cattle they had come for were bewitched. They sat in the darkness without speaking, some touching the small pieces of root and bone which they wore for protection. Then, pulling their blankets more closely around their bodies, they went with Diko into the bushes and bedded down for the night.

Their limbs cold and stiff from the damp, they rose as soon as it was light and, disgruntled, stood stretching themselves and looking around, when, through the gray morning mist, the men saw cattle: first a black-and-white stippled ox, then a few heifers, then more, a small herd of oxen.

Pale and ghostly against the soft gray of the mimosa thorn, the cattle moved slowly down the lower side of the ravine. "Let them come to drink," Diko whispered urgently, for then it would be easy to drive them over the river. The appearance of the cattle called for a change in his plan, and Diko made an instant decision. They would chase this small group across the river, after which he would let two men round them up while he and the rest of the men went for the main herd. They would have to hurry before the other cattle also came to drink.

Tense with excitement, the men waited. This was what they had come for: cattle! They watched the silent forms moving between the thorn trees not more than fifty paces from where they stood. When the animals disappeared behind a line of dense growth, Diko stole forward to a thick, scrubby bush close to the bank and beckoned the men to come. Now, from a crouched position, they could look through the bushes and see the riverbank itself. At any minute the cattle would appear again.

The bushes separated, and the black-and-white stippled ox came out onto the bank, the herd following slowly. Through the drifting mist which covered the ground, Diko and his men counted in tens on one hand. Not a sound could be heard as the animals crossed the stretch of firm sand. So silent was the ravine it seemed that nothing was awake, nothing except a solitary dove, whose repeated calling came from the bushes nearby, and even that soon ceased.

While the cattle were wading through the rocky shallows, Diko crept back to the place where he had tethered his ox and returned, leading Black Water by a rawhide rope. To make sure that the herd would be taken by surprise, he waited until all the animals were drinking. Then he signaled his men.

Spreading out on the bank, the men began to creep up behind the herd, while Diko stood waiting on the edge of the thickets. Braced for a sudden uproar, he kept his hand firmly on the tether lest the animal bolt. What if the other cattle were to come now? he thought. All would be lost because they would run away in a headlong flight and scatter.

Why were the men moving so slowly? They should have taken care of this lot by now. The very stillness was disquieting. Again he became aware of the sound of the dove, louder this time, strangely persistent. He saw the men reach the water's edge. In another moment they would be brandishing their sticks and shouting at the cattle.

The next he knew, a piercing whistle shattered the silence. Diko froze. The men stopped dead in their tracks; the cattle lifted their heads and began to mill and face about. Another shrill whistle from the opposite bank, and the herd, moving as one, came slowly out of the water toward the men. They fled back across the sand. Diko escaped with his ox up the side of the ravine.

Suddenly something moved in the scrub. He heard warning snorts from Black Water, a cracking in the undergrowth, and a huge black-and-white bull pushed its way through. Wherever he turned, there were cattle coming slowly out of the bushes. He ran down again, sweeping along the men who had been behind him. They rushed back into the open, only to find themselves trapped by the cattle from the river. The small herd was moving across the bank, led by the black-and-white stippled ox with pendent horns. Slowly and menacingly the cattle advanced from all sides, drawing the ring tighter and tighter.

On the other side of the river Anta stood up. Putting a small bone whistle to his mouth, he gave two hard, shrill blasts. The herd paused for an instant, waiting for their leader. Then, with a roar as from the mouths of lions, the cattle closed in. Running to the water, Anta strained to get a better look. He could hear the fearful cries of the men over the lowing and bellowing of the cattle, but through the mist and the dust that enveloped them, he saw nothing.

It was over within minutes. In the silence that came after, the old herdsman joined Anta, and together they crossed the river. When the dust settled, they saw that the cattle were walking off, leaving behind the trampled and gored bodies of Diko and his ten men. A little apart, as if he had charged his attackers, Black Water lay dead, his neck and shoulders soaked with blood. They saw Big Forest stop, sniff at the body, and turn away to join the herd.

Anta was appalled. He could not look at the crushed bodies on the ground. The worst of it was Diko. For all his wrongdoing he was a brother.

A great sob burst from him. The old man saw his anguish. "He would always have been a thorn under your foot," he stated. "In the end he would have tried to kill you. It is a good thing for the people that he is dead. Son of Khwane, you did well, you and your ox." Then, talking more to himself than to Anta, he said, "It is ever so. When a man wishes harm to cattle, the evil will return to strike him."

The old herdsman was silent for a time before he spoke again. If Diko had disclosed the whereabouts of the herd to Oba, such a thing could happen again because Oba would send men to find out why the others had not returned. "We must find another place for the cattle," he told Anta. "It is time to take them to new grazing, and it is safer. But we may not have to go far." Diko had come upon them by chance, and in this whole maze of ravines it was unlikely that they would be discovered again. The most secure places were higher up in the mountains in the chasms among the steep crags, but there was no need for them to choose a hiding place so difficult of approach.

While the cattle were making their leisurely way up the ravine, Anta and the old man crossed the river again, stepping on stones in the water to reach the opposite bank. For a long while they followed the rivercourse, noting the drinking places, and, finding a good one, began to climb the bushy slopes. Toward midday they saw what they were looking for: a small open plateau shaded by acacia trees and hidden from view by rocks and thorn. That same day they moved the herd to the new sanctuary across the river, and the next morning Anta and Big Forest started for home.

All the way down the mountain his mood was somber, his mind heavy with thoughts of what had happened. He would tell his father how they had turned the cattle on Diko and the other men, but his father would have to find some way of explaining Diko's death to the people if the secret of the herd were to be kept. He hoped he had done what his father would have wanted. The herd was safe. The people could get on with their peaceful lives. Diko was gone. Yet he could not forget the sight of his body.

Leaving the thorn country far behind, he traveled with his ox over the rolling hills, his eyes fixed on the faint blue line of the distant mountains. Each day brought him closer to those towering blue ridges behind Nkomkobé Hill. At last Nkomkobé itself loomed up on the plains. In the late afternoon, when the hills around him were already in shadow, he saw Nkomkobé bathed in sun. As he drew nearer, the green of the hillside turned soft and luminous against the deep blue of the stony ridges. Anta laid his hand lightly on his ox. Soon, from the top of that high hill, he could look around and see the sky touching the broad green slopes on every side. His heart sang. They were home.

pronunciation guide

ANTA	**AHN**-tah
BALAKAZI	bah-lah-**KAH**-zee
DIKO	**DEE**-koh
ENXHELE	en-**KEH**-leh
ÉWE	**EEAH**-weh
GEDJA	**GED**-jah
GONOGONO	**GON**-oh-**GON**-oh
HLATIKULU	shlah-tee-**KOO**-loo
HLUBI	**SHLOO**-bee
IGQIRA	ih-**GIH**-rah
IXHWELE	ih-**KWEH**-leh
KHWANE	**KWAH**-nee
KHOIKHOI	**KHOY**-**KHOY**
KOTONGO	kuh-**TON**-goh
LAF' INDUNE' ELIHLE LAKOWETHU, LIBINZWA LIKRELE LOMONA	lahf-in-**DOO**-neh eh-**LEE**-leh lah-koh-**VEE**-too, lih-**BINZ**-vah lih-**KREH**-leh loh-**MOH**-nah
LOLOMBELA	loh-lom-**BEH**-lah
MABONI	muh-**BOH**-nee
MABOPE	muh-**BOH**-peh
MANZÁNYAMA	mahn-**ZAHN**-yah-mah
MLANDU	muh-**LAHN**-doo
MLONJI	muh-**LON**-jee

131

MTOBA	muh-**TOH**-bah
MVENYANE	muh-ven-**YAH**-nee
NAMBA	**NAHM**-bah
NGUBENGCUKA	en-goo-ben-**KOO**-kah
NKOMKOBÉ	en-kom-**KOH-BEH**
NOMALISO	noh-mah-**LEE**-soh
NUNGE	**NOON**-ghee
OBA	**OH**-bah
PINDA	**PIN**-dah
SIBI	**SEE**-bee
SIDALO	sih-**DAH**-loh
SIYAVUMA	see-yah-**VOO**-mah
SONTO	**SON**-toh
SONWABA	son-**VAH**-bah
TANDEKA	tahn-**DEE**-kah
THUBISI	too-**BEE**-see
uBHAYILAM	ooh-**BAH**-yih-lahm
uGQUMA BABALEKE	ooh-**GOO**-mah bah-bah-**LEH**-keh
UMAKHULU	ooh-mah-**KOO**-loo
UMATUTA	ooh-mah-**TOO**-tah
UMCELU	oom-**CHEH**-loo
VUKILI	voo-**KEE**-lee
VUKUTHU	voo-**KOO**-too
XHOSA	**KOH**-sah
YAKWAXHEGO	yuhk-vah-**SHWAY**-goh
YALO	**YAH**-loh